About the Author

Nod Ghosh was born in Birmingham and currently lives in Christchurch, New Zealand, where she works as a medical laboratory scientist specialising in the diagnosis of cancers. Her short stories and flash fiction have been widely published in journals and anthologies, and her work has been listed for awards including the Bath Novella-in-Flash Award and the Wallace Arts Trust Alternative Bindings Competition. She has had four previous novellas published: *The Crazed Wind* (2018), *Filthy Sucre* (2020), *Toy Train* (2021) and *Throw a Seven* (2023).

T0021773

The Two-Tailed Snake

NOD GHOSH

Fairlight Books

First published by Fairlight Books 2023

Fairlight Books
Summertown Pavilion, 18–24 Middle Way, Oxford, OX2 7LG

A CIP catalogue record for this book is available from the
British Library

1 2 3 4 5 6 7 8 9 10

ISBN 978-1-914148-42-2

www.fairlightbooks.com

Printed and bound in Great Britain by Clays Ltd.

Designed by Sara Wood

Illustrated by Sam Kalda

MIX
Paper from
responsible sources
FSC® C018072

*To those who endure living through
troubled times, then and now.*

List of Characters

Joya Guho
Baba – Mr Guho, Joya's father, a police officer
Ma – Mrs Guho, Joya's mother

Maia – Joya's best friend
Boromama – Maia's wealthy uncle
Mamima – Maia's aunt and Boromama's wife

Yusef – Joya's Muslim neighbour and friend
Faarooq Uncle – Yusef's father
Rukhsana Khala – Yusef's mother

Master-Moshai – Joya's teacher when she is a young child
Headmaster – head of the school when Joya is a teenager

Tiya Mashi – Joya's maternal aunt, from the west, near Noamundi
Mesho-Moshai – Joya's uncle and Tiya Mashi's husband
Aroti – Joya's cousin, Tiya Mashi's eldest daughter
Shanti – Joya's cousin, Tiya Mashi's second-eldest daughter
Priya – Joya's cousin, Tiya Mashi's youngest daughter

Chondon – driver for Tiya Mashi and Mesho-Moshai
Neha – elderly cook at Tiya Mashi and Mesho-Moshai's house

Shom Mamu – Joya's distant uncle, who employs her in his factory near New Market
Lohith – Joya's manager at the factory

Mary D'Costa – Ma's friend
Audrey Alvares – Ma's friend

Snakes I

Snakes come in many forms, yah! I've heard it said we are good company when we perform our duty without scheming and conspiring to pervert the course of justice.

I've heard that you perceive us as good or evil according to your needs. Ah, the hubris of humanity!

There are kraits and green tree vipers, whose venom will become beneficial in time. The gods know we serpents will be valuable one day, our defence used to create antivenoms and other gifts to mankind. Those with a love of ophiology and studying reptiles in general will nurture us, especially where there is a profit to be made. You may call me cynical, but I am only an observer, a scaly one with bead-like eyes who has glimpsed the future.

And what of anguine prophets? There are as many stories told about us serpents as the ones we tell ourselves.

A snake-god, Ananta-Shesha, circles the world. All-seeing. All-knowing. Ananta hears prophecies about white serpents who cross the ocean, who are vanquished in battle and return to salt water, defeated. Ananta hears it all.

And what of sanguine prophesiers, who sit at firesides passing tales to their children and children's children, frightening them by foretelling their misfortunes? I have heard so much said by those who know so little.

There is a legend whispered among the initiated, but perhaps not whispered often enough, or loudly enough. It is said that if one slaughters a snake, death will follow. Make a snake angry, insult us or show disrespect, and a curse will lead to sickness and calamity. We may not act immediately, but bad fortune will find you. Eventually.

There are benevolent snake-deities within the sub-pantheon. Those who support the weight of the planets with their multitudinous heads humbly accept offerings of eggs and milk from worshippers. The Supreme Being, the trinity of higher gods, the Trimurti of Lord Vishnu, Lord Brahma and Lord Shiva will bless those such as Ananta, whose yawn may cause the earth to shiver.

There is Vasuki, who dwells on Lord Shiva's neck, who stirs his tail in the oceans and whips up an ambrosia of immortality.

There is Manasadevi, the queen of snakes. She is also the god of poison. Her eyes are as black as the queen of Ishkapon or Chiraton. But are they truly as black as spades or clubs? Or is there a glint of diamond in them that reveals her true heart?

And there is Kāliya, feared by many, who lurks in the black waters of the river, and is known for terrorising infant gods.

We are not all divine, but many snakes hold the power of divination. I could tell you how the earth will end. We reside in the last of the four ages of the epoch, but all is not as it appears in the scriptures. If only you knew how to read the *Puranas* accurately, yah!

There are many of us. Innocent snakes. Corrupt snakes. Dead snakes. Comical snakes. There are snakes that reproduce without coitus. Try that if you can. It's been done, I'm told.

We are not all literal. Some are divine energy, coiled tight as a spring, waiting to be awoken so your consciousness may be raised.

We shed our skins and are reborn, for which we are revered and envied.

And we are abused.

There are fakirs who coax defanged snakes to dance. Some sew our mouths together into narrow slits so only the tongue protrudes. Such cruelty! Such depravity! We dance in and out of wicker baskets, the thin wail of a pungi reed pipe creating the illusion of mesmerisation. In reality, we have been subdued by means of intoxicating herbs. At least it takes some of the pain away. Ahhhh!

There are snakes that curl into a ball and disappear when they hear the thwack of a policeman's lathi, only to follow the gullible man and lure him later with intoxicating offers. And though snakes divine or simple may admonish these deviants until they slither away guilt-ridden and forlorn, they will always return if there is a chance of a few coins to be gained.

We know there are good and bad among us, and those like me, who are indifferent.

There is one among us, a snake with two tails, who is a man, is a serpent, no, a man really – perhaps a bit of both. Listen closely to this tale. And in parallel, you will hear another story.

Perhaps it is two tales in one.

Shorbonaash

On the morning everything changed, Joya's mother cried, 'Shorbonaash!'

Shorbonaash meant the destruction of all things. A laying waste to everything that was known.

Shorbonaash set cartwheels turning in Joya's chest.

Shorbonaash was said with the blast of a hundred atomic bombs, far worse than those that had recently dropped on Japan.

Shorbonaash resonated with the force of Lord Shiva holding Parvati's hand, as the gods ran circles around the world, leaving destruction in their wake.

And then silence.

Joya wandered into every room of the tiny house, looking for her mother. She found Ma in the garden, sitting next to the patch of earth where vegetables and herbs grew. She was weeping.

'What happened?' Joya placed an arm around her mother's trembling shoulders. There were clumps of dirt in her hair, as if she'd clutched it with her soiled hands.

Ma said nothing.

'Are you all right?' Joya wondered why her father hadn't responded to the calamity, whatever it was. She pulled her mother to her full height. 'Where is Baba?'

'Why? He's gone, of course,' Ma replied, wiping wet eyes with her forearm, smearing more earth over her face. 'Now help me. We have no time to waste. You will be late for school.'

Joya led her mother into the house.

Gone could mean all manner of things. Had Baba been called away urgently? Was he needed on duty?

Was there an emergency in the neighbourhood that needed his assistance?

Or could Ma and Baba have quarrelled? Joya's parents often had disagreements, but they always settled their differences.

So where had he *gone*? Joya didn't know what to think.

For the moment, though, there was a school bag to pack: a comic she'd borrowed from her friend Maia, her mathematics exercise book, some greasy paratha from the freshly made stack in the glass-lidded bowl on the table and a catapult her neighbour Yusef had made that she simply *had* to show Maia.

But how could everything carry on as normal after Ma's *shorbonaash*?

BEFORE
EVERYTHING
CHANGES

Purebred

Joya's mother packed the brand-new steel tiffin carrier with luchi and spiced potatoes for her daughter to take. It would be unthinkable for a guest to arrive somewhere empty-handed.

'But Ma,' Joya said, 'We're visiting Maia's Boromama.'

'Even more reason you should take. But you must bring the tiffin carrier back. Your father has just bought this from New Market. It is for your school lunches. Baba will be upset if you lose it.'

'It's beautiful. I'll take care of it.' Joya kissed her mother's cheek and tucked the container in her rucksack. She skipped out of the house as she heard the car horn.

Joya's friend Maia enthusiastically invited friends to her wealthy uncle's home. She acted as if the splendour of her Boromama's house elevated her. Joya liked going, though she found the journey uncomfortable. It was hot inside the black beetle-shaped car, even with the fan blowing. Their driver dodged carts pulled by skinny horses, trams, buses and thousands of bicycles as they edged their way past Howrah station, across the bridge to the leafy suburb where Maia's uncle lived.

Joya loved the place. It was good to jump out of the car as soon as the surly driver parked in front of the pearl-white house. So much space! Joya would run along the gully beside the house. Back and forth and back again, until she was out of breath, her shalwar kameez soaked in sweat. Maia would run behind her shouting, 'Slow down! Slow down! Wait for me.'

On entering the house, Joya had to remember to show Maia's uncle the respect he was due. She'd crouch to touch his feet then lift her fingers to her forehead. Boromama was much fatter than his sister, Maia's mother, and Joya's head often brushed against his round belly as she completed the pronaam.

'Na, na, na!' the man would say each time, pinching Joya's cheek. 'Don't have to do that.' But Joya knew he was as obligated to refuse her gesture as she was obliged to perform it despite his protestations. 'And which one are you?' he'd ask every time, peering through his thick glasses, cupping her chin in his hand as if performing a medical examination. 'Such good bone structure.'

'This is Joya,' Maia would say. 'The policeman's daughter. Remember? She's my school friend.' Then Boromama would pull away, as if something sticky had exuded from Joya's skin and contaminated his fingers.

The first time Maia had invited Joya to her uncle's homestead, she'd explained, 'Boromama is the family patriarch.' She'd pointed to portraits of various white-robed ancestors. 'That means he's the boss,' she'd continued, opening her aunt's wooden almari and rolling paan with the expertise of a street-seller. 'Don't let anyone see your red tongue afterwards, or they'll know we took khoyer and paan from Mamima's cupboard.'

Boromama lived in the whitewashed mansion with stone serpents guarding the entrance, while Maia's own family lived somewhere more modest on the other side of the river. According to Maia, that difference bore no relation to the fact that her father worked for the Civil Service while Boromama *did what he did* (it wasn't clear to Joya what that was). The hierarchy was inalienable, as if Boromama had been born destined for greatness.

Joya contemplated the differences between the places where they lived as she bit into the paan leaf Maia had folded into a triangular parcel. She imagined filling her friend's house with water, and pouring that water into the uncle's dwelling. She reckoned it would take four refills. And if Maia's garden were a rug, it might take fifty such rugs to cover the lands that surrounded Boromama's mansion, including the gully where Joya loved running.

Joya estimated that using the water trick to calculate the difference between Maia's house and an even smaller one like hers or her neighbour Yusef's would take another multiple of four.

Back and forth, measure and pour.

Their teacher once said Joya had a good head for such things. She could *estimate values* better than anyone in class.

But Joya hadn't thought about any of that when playing kabaddi in the gully with Maia's younger cousins, or peeping through the bamboo screen where older cousins drank whiskey and threw dice, cigarette smoke haloing their heads.

Boromama's house came with a set of grandparents and three gruesome-looking cats.

'They don't bite, silly,' Maia said when a curious creature jumped up to sniff Joya's leg as she handed the new tiffin carrier to the cook.

'They look so strange,' Joya replied.

Maia said the reason their faces were squashed, like the balushahis you could buy at Vikat's Emporium of Sweets, was because the creatures were purebred.

'What is purebred?' Joya asked.

'Like us,' Maia replied. 'Bengalis, who only marry Bengalis.' She looked behind her. 'And caste marries within caste.' She stopped in the corridor and tapped Joya's head as if commending her. 'Purebred, and *first class*.'

'That's a good thing?'

'Of course.'

'And mixing is bad?'

'Yah! Why breed mongrels?' Maia glanced back at the open kitchen door. 'Let's conduct a séance. We'll ask the spirits.'

'Okay, yah!' Joya covered her embarrassment about the uncertainty over her own pedigree as they returned to the lounge. She turned her attention instead to conjuring a ghost from thin air using an upturned glass. Joya thought the game a little silly. Why would anyone want to talk to dead people?

It seemed that the spirits were unwilling to answer such complex questions that day, focusing instead on whether the girls' future husbands would have fair or dark skin, be left-handed or lame.

Joya sometimes wondered if her friend was too forthright in her opinions. She didn't have the confidence to question Maia. Her father would be able to explain things more clearly than she. But

23

Baba never went to Maia's house, and certainly never came to Boromama's mansion.

Through a half-open door, Joya had once heard her father telling Ma, 'I find this whole caste business so distasteful.'

'Yes. So unnecessary, ogo,' Ma had replied, addressing Baba by the endearment she only used in private. 'And why we must remain silent about how—'

But the door had closed. Joya hadn't heard the rest.

There was a large swamp next to the gully in Boromama's garden. Joya liked throwing stones into the murk. She and Maia would listen to a plop followed by soundless travel to an unknowable depth, where unfathomable creatures lurked.

Maia's grandfather had caught several koi maach in the swamp that day. They'd watched the cook de-fin the creatures while they were still alive. Then, mercifully, she'd tossed them into bubbling oil. Joya initially refused to eat the fish, but eventually hunger and curiosity overcame her. Though delicious, the fish dish wasn't the best item on the table that day. The cook had warmed the luchi and fried potatoes and placed them on a brass thali. The new stainless-steel canister had been washed, dried and returned to Joya's rucksack.

Wrapping some aloo bhaja in one of Ma's flatbreads, Joya closed her eyes and savoured the food.

Celebrations

Food was very important for Joya's family – it lay at the heart of every celebration. Her mother prepared feasts for birthdays and anniversaries. She made buttery breads, aromatic savouries and milky sweets, and served them with succulent fruits. Their little house was filled with laughter. They'd light oil lamps. Baba said they were blessed to have such good fortune.

Ma, Baba and Joya teased one another, but it was done with humour. Ma had a stock of customs and sayings, which she'd acquired from goodness knows where. Joya's only aunt and cousins weren't quite so superstitious. But Ma's maxims and proverbs were like unbreakable laws.

Never give anyone money at night.

Never repair your clothes while wearing them.

Never stare at a distressed person.

Never cast your eyes on an egg before a school exam.

Never consume aubergine on the first Thursday of the month.

Never accept a gift without first refusing it.

Never, never, never.

There were so many decrees that Joya had trouble remembering them. Baba teased his wife about their number and complexity, but Ma smiled her crooked smile, relishing the attention.

Not all Ma's rules began with *never*, but the ones that were prefaced by *always* were harder to obey.

Some were easy enough to follow. Avoiding begoon once a month was no hardship.

Some of Ma's pronouncements straddled the line between superstition and the sacred. It was difficult to know whether there was a divine basis to her practices involving water. Joya once read there were three hundred and thirty million different deities in and around India. Perhaps one of them demanded the bizarre rituals Ma practised. So Joya indulged her mother by looking at the sun through a stream of water poured from a pot to strengthen her eyes. She rigorously followed the rules regarding water sources in their tiny home, paying heed to which were regarded as less clean and therefore less sacred than the alternatives.

Religion was everywhere.

Ma built shrines in the strangest places. Joya and her father might stumble upon a garlanded image in the washroom or beside the rice sack. They treated them with respect. If their hands brushed against an icon, they touched their fingertips to their forehead and chest, for who knew what catastrophe might befall them if they didn't counter such transgressions with a remedy?

No matter how hungry they might have been in other ways when awaiting Baba's next pay packet, their spiritual appetites were always satisfied.

If they weren't preparing rangoli patterns for Diwali, perhaps they were wishing Christian friends well for Easter. Near Yuletide, Baba attended talks at the chapel near the police outpost where he was stationed, and brought home tales from distant lands and occasional small gifts.

One year, Ma listened to the city's bishop deliver a sermon at St John's with her friend Mary D'Costa, and took holy bread with Audrey Alvares, but was obliged to forgo the blood of Christ, for fear of arriving home tipsy.

That same year, when Ramadan drew to an end, there was a festive atmosphere, as Eid would follow soon. Joya played with her neighbour Yusef on the flattened earth behind their homes. She peered through the window at Yusef's mother, Rukhsana Khala, busily chopping, paring and stirring.

'What's she making?' Joya asked.

'Kharouf mahshi,' Yusef replied. Joya remembered the richly spiced mutton dish the neighbours had served in previous years.

Rukhsana often worked deep into the night, up to her elbows in pastry. There had been times Ma and Joya were recruited to roll and flatten the little balls of dough. Yusef had asked to help one year, but Rukhsana had scolded her son for popping raw balls of dough into his mouth.

'It'll make you sick!' she had yelled. 'And why aren't you fasting?'

'Amma, the sun set an hour ago,' Yusef had replied. 'When is iftar?'

'Not yet!' his mother replied.

Yusef managed to sneak another blob of dough into his mouth, since they would not officially break their fast until every task was completed even though the sun had set hours earlier. Eventually, to keep his fingers away from the dough, Faarooq Uncle took his son to the mosque where, Joya was told, the men coordinated the Zakat-al-Fitr charitable donations.

At Durga Puja, Ma, Baba and Joya wore their best clothes, gave gifts to the neighbourhood children and visited the local pandals. They were mesmerised by the intricacy of the temporary structures that rose above their heads. Some were three or four storeys high, adorned with coloured lights surrounding images of Durga with her multiple arms and startling eyes.

For her birthday one year, Audrey Alvares made Joya a candy-studded gingerbread house, reminiscent of the witch's hut in *Hansel and Gretel*. She'd saved it for days, and then shared chunks with Yusef and Maia.

'We're so lucky our parents won't send us out into the woods because they can't feed us,' Joya told her friends.

'That nonsense is just for little kids, yah?' Maia had replied, pushing a sugar windowpane into her mouth. It occurred to Joya that Maia had little understanding of what it meant to go without. And why would she? Maia's family were fortunate. They never anticipated the next pay packet in the way Joya's family did.

Joya knew how hard her parents worked to make those special occasions magical. It wasn't always easy to count her blessings, but she tried nonetheless.

Wrong or Right

Joya was exceptionally good at mathematics.

Her mother insisted on calling mathematics *onko*, which Joya thought was a babyish word. *Onko* implied sums a small child would do, not something for someone who'd just turned fourteen and was faster and more accurate than all her classmates.

Her father always encouraged Joya to work hard at school.

'School isn't hard!' she'd counter.

'Everything is a game to you, shona-moni.'

Baba was right. Everything *did* seem like a game to Joya, though a challenging one at times.

She loved writing as well.

When she was younger, Master-Moshai, the teacher at the little school, had said Joya's handwriting was the best in the class.

First class, as Maia would say.

First in class.

The best.

Master-Moshai had said she'd be the first pupil to try the fountain pens that were locked in a cupboard. But before that, she'd need to practise her letters with pencil on paper, so she could start by inking over the graphite *orw-ahr-horshoi-diggoi* with a precious iridium-tipped nib.

But pencil and paper were more expensive than chalk for a slate, and somehow other children – including Maia – overtook her with pen and ink.

When she was older, while Ma worried about teaching Joya how to wash her monthly rags in cold water so the stains wouldn't set, Baba looked over her mathematics textbooks in awe.

'You are doing *calculus* now?' he asked her one day.

'Only the top class,' Joya said.

'And you will be best student in the top class,' Baba replied. It wasn't a command, more a divination.

'What is this *calculus-thalculus*?' Ma interrupted. 'Will it help her find a good husband?' she asked her own good husband.

'Array! A bright girl such as this, and you worry about marriage?' Baba frowned at Joya's mother. 'She could attend university. Husbands galore will fight for her hand, but in good time.'

'She might have degree and diploma growing from her head like a pair of horns, but who will want to marry an old maid of twenty-five who is too clever to know when to shut up and listen?'

'Mamuni, you yourself have no BA, but still you are far too clever to know when to be quiet!' Though Baba was smiling and had used Ma's pet name, Joya sensed a quarrel brewing. She hoped it wouldn't escalate.

Sometimes Joya overheard her parents talking late at night. They weren't exactly fighting, but their interactions were far from jovial, spiked with undercurrents of fear. They'd whisper words such as *corruption*, *extortion* and *nepotism*; ideas she didn't understand. And when a character called the *two-tailed snake* was mentioned, their murmurings sounded ominous, threatening.

Joya had once asked Maia if she'd heard of the snake. Her friend had said, 'Don't be silly. That stuff is all made up, yah?'

Joya slipped out of the room. Perhaps Yusef would be home. She could talk to her neighbour about films they'd like to see, if they could ever find money for a ticket. Perhaps he had finished fashioning the cricket bat he'd been working on for weeks. Yusef was always making something.

Joya wandered towards the flattened earth behind their homes, and Yusef ran to meet her. He was almost as tall as she was. His limbs scissored this way and that as he approached.

'Why the glum face, yah?' the boy asked.

'It's nothing,' Joya said, even though it was something.

Faarooq Uncle and Rukhsana Khala were tilling the soil in the tiny strip of land where they grew vegetables. It was only the width and length of a sari, but every year Yusef's parents produced a crop of aubergine, okra and tomatoes – buckets of them – which they shared with the neighbours. Joya could hear them exchanging mocking words. The way they teased each other reminded Joya of her own parents: they always had something to say, but most of it was in jest. Even their harshest words were spiced with laughter.

'What nothing? This is not nothing!' Yusef pinched Joya's cheeks and pulled them into a forced smile. 'Really. Tell me what happened. Did you fight with the queen of Ishkapon?'

'No. Nothing like that,' Joya said, pulling away, though the smile remained. Yusef's nickname for Maia related to the Bibi, the queen of spades. Maia often lost games where being dealt the black queen spelled trouble. The name made Joya laugh.

When they were younger, Maia, Joya and Yusef had played together regularly. Then Maia began excluding Yusef. Perhaps she didn't want to play with a boy. Maia and Yusef had been arguing lately. But their bickering was *not* peppered with laughter.

Joya had pointed out to Maia that she and Yusef would never make a good married couple, because they couldn't resolve their differences.

'You think *that* is the only reason we could not marry?' Maia had said, looking incredulous. 'Not that I would want to marry that bōkā fool.'

'Well, no,' Joya had said, not wishing to sound naive. 'There are other reasons, of course,' she'd added, though in reality she wasn't sure why such absolute rules existed about who was allowed to marry whom. But it was true. Maia and Yusef had argued more than they'd had civil conversations in the last few months, causing a rift that affected the three of them, friends who had been loyal to each other for years.

If they weren't quarrelling about the superiority of a love story such as *Zindaji* over a murder mystery like *Khazanchi*, they'd have heated debates about whether pointed gourds were better fried or broiled.

But potol bhaja is the only way to eat such a vegetable.

Rubbish! You should simmer potol in milk and ghee. There is no other way to enjoy it.

The stupid thing was that neither Maia nor Yusef, as far as Joya knew, had been to the cinema to see *Zindaji* or *Khazanchi*. And both loved potol, regardless of how it was prepared.

More recently, their altercations had intensified. They quoted newspaper articles and argued about current affairs. Joya found it hard to follow what they were discussing, and to understand who actually stood for what. They'd mention words she'd heard on the radiogram. *Curfew, Quit India* and *Do or Die*. She tried to make sense of what they were saying, but it was difficult when they seemed to change their viewpoint every time they talked about those things.

'What is it, then?' Yusef persevered. 'Why is your face as long as a potol?'

'Well…' Joya hesitated. 'It's not as if I never want to marry.'

'Marry? Who is talking of marriage now?'

'Yah, marry. Ma would probably have me matched with a fat husband who constantly burps and farts by now if it weren't for Baba.'

'Your father is a wise man.' They were sitting against the back wall of the compound.

'He is. I wish Ma would see things the same way.'

'Maybe. But there could be a reason she wants to see you settled.'

'What reason? Why think of marriage now, when we should be playing, watching films and finishing our studies?' Joya drew her knees to her chest.

'There's a lot happening in the world.' Yusef sounded serious. The rosewood trees that surrounded the cluster of small dwellings stood tall and still in the windless air. He walked to the smallest one, a tree they'd often climbed when they were younger, and returned with a little stone. He rubbed the dirt off the surface with his thumbs. 'See this?' He pointed to the smooth top. 'This is everyday life. The things you fret about daily. They take some work, but can easily be managed without bumps and difficulties.'

Joya listened in silence.

'This,' Yusef said, flipping the stone over to reveal a pocked and creviced underside covered in mud, 'is what happens underneath.'

'What do you mean?'

'There is much happening if you look beneath the surface. Your mother might want to see you under someone's care before things become more unsettled.'

'Why?' Joya asked. 'I'm under *their* care.'

'Your father is a police officer.'

'So, why does that matter?'

'Because of what's happening.'

Joya often became frustrated when Yusef spoke this way, as if he were much wiser than she, even though they were the same age.

'Why? What's happening?' she challenged.

'Things are changing,' he said. 'Don't you read the newspapers?'

'I want to,' she said. 'But Baba says I shouldn't worry about political business. He says I'm clever and need to concentrate on my studies.'

'There are different sorts of clever, Joya.' Yusef glanced at his mother. Rukhsana Khala had risen from the vegetable plot, and was sprinkling water from a metal bowl onto the seedlings Faarooq Uncle had patted into the soil. 'Some things look the same on the surface, but underneath they're shifting. Change is coming.'

'Why do you talk in riddles? Is this why you and Maia constantly argue?'

'Maia may not be as good at onko as you are, but she's not stupid. She knows things will change and why.'

Joya was surprised. Recently, Yusef had behaved as if everything Maia said was wrong, and only he knew what was right.

'Tell me,' she said, 'have you heard of the two-tailed snake?'

'No,' he said, 'but the changes that are coming are far scarier than any snake.'

'What will change?' she demanded.

'Everything,' her friend replied.

The Secret

Joya discovered her friend's secret the summer before everything changed.

Maia and Joya were leaning against a neem tree, chewing on blades of grass, when Maia bent over and whispered in her ear. What she said made Joya realise she didn't know her friend as well as she thought she did.

'How long?' she whispered, though the chances of anyone else hearing them in that part of the playground were remote.

'One year.'

'*One year?*' Joya screeched, forgetting to whisper.

'Yes. A year,' Maia replied evenly.

How was that possible?

How could Joya not have known?

How could Maia have been in love with a *boy*, without her parents knowing? Surely their schoolteachers, who had eyes like eagles, would have discovered what was happening and put an end to it?

And what a name he had!

Not one of the Abhijeets or Lalits or Rajus, trainee doctors and lawyers and engineers whom Maia's parents hinted would make a formal proposal via their fathers within the year.

Not one of the Dilips or Bachhus or Prabirs who congregated in Maia's Boromama's house, drinking liquor with her cousins, playing cards and talking about *political business*, who might have tempted her if she'd felt rebellious.

No.

This boy possessed a very different sort of name.

Did Maia have no sense of the danger such a union posed?

Huh!

Maia, who'd said *Bengalis only marry Bengalis.* How long ago had that been? Was it said for the benefit of eavesdropping ears? So this mashi or that mesho might think *What a good girl our Maia is.* Where had they been at the time? At Maia's uncle's place? Had her friend been concealing her liaison with *this boy* by implying she'd never break the rules?

What else had she said?

You think that *is the only reason we could not marry*, when speaking of Yusef, as if Joya didn't understand their religions' differences meant little except in large matters.

Caste must marry within caste. How terrible Maia had made Joya feel. She *knew* there was some mystery surrounding how Joya's mother and father had been brought together, and still she'd laboured the issue.

Details about Ma and Baba's people were glossed over or changed with each telling. Joya had never known her paternal relatives. When she was little, she'd been told they'd all died. Later she surmised the situation was more complicated. Sometimes adults revealed more than they should when conversing in the presence of children. They confidently believed youngsters were incapable of understanding, simply because they didn't want the child to know, especially when they spoke of breaking unbreakable rules.

Thus Joya had discovered she had mixed lineage.

Caste marries within caste. Except when human attraction intervenes.

Ma and Baba were different, but similar.

One had an ancestry of traders and merchants; the other warriors and rulers.

Both were Bengali, from the same land, of the same blood.

One was superstitious and set store by proverbs; the other was practical and rational.

Both believed that poor choices must be balanced by good deeds.

One thought marriage took precedence over a girl's education; the other did not.

Both believed marriage should be with someone loyal and trustworthy.

But this boy Maia had chosen!

This boy was not only from a different racial group; he may as well have been a different species.

'Well, say something,' Maia pleaded. 'Don't sit there like a statue.'

'A whole year?' Joya pressed her friend.

'Yes. Well, eleven months and three weeks.'

'And you are telling me now! After eleven months and three weeks.' Joya steadied her voice. 'Why bother at all? It feels as if you've been lying to me.' She wanted to quash the bubbling hurt, the pain that added sharps and flats to the tune of her words.

'An omission. Not a lie.'

'It *is* a lie.' Joya hated the cry in her voice, but could do little to suppress it.

'A white lie.'

Oh, how apt.

White.

Joya was upset. She wanted to repay the hurt, abandon her friend, but she needed to know what had happened – something she'd been too blind to see.

So they talked, Maia's tone oscillating between excitement and earnestness. There was a reason the proverbial cat was leaping out of its bag at that moment. What was the saying they'd learned in English class?

A friend in need is a friend indeed.

Maia had been communicating with this Michael Smith for a year, after she'd enrolled in a club he'd organised.

'What sort of club?' Joya asked, expecting perhaps chess or badminton. But if so, why had Joya not known about it? Wasn't Maia one of her closest friends?

'It's a poetry club,' Maia replied. 'We're reading "Kubla Khan".'

'What is that? Is it from the Quran?' Joya asked.

'Of course not. It's a poem by Samuel Taylor Coleridge.'

'And why do you need to join a club to read such poetry?'

'We discuss it. Write our own pieces too. Did you know that particular poem was inspired by a dream Coleridge had after he took opium?'

'Array baap-re! So now you are taking bhang with this boyfriend I didn't know you had until five minutes ago.'

'Not hashish. Opium. And *we* didn't take drugs. The poet did. But anyway, will you help me?'

Maia's secret boyfriend was one she had not yet met in real life.

White.

How do you know?

I have his photo.

Their interactions were all through letters. It was a very cerebral love affair.

Not just a non-Bengali.

A Britisher.

What would Boromama say if he knew?

The details of how Maia had found the poetry club through answering an advert in the community hall were glossed over. She had a more immediate problem.

Maia's mother had intercepted a letter addressed to her daughter before the daughter herself could secrete it away. Mentions of *pleasure-domes* and *deep romantic chasms* had resulted in apoplexy.

Maia needed someone to receive Michael's letters for her.

That's where Joya came into the equation.

Joya was honoured Maia could share such a dangerous secret with her.

The Magician

One of Joya and Maia's favourite pastimes involved telling each other their earliest memories. The game alternated between honest truth and pure imagination, and there was an arbitrary points system.

The last time they'd played had been at Maia's uncle's grand house. When Joya arrived at Boromama's house that day, she had expected things would be no different from her previous visit.

Perhaps she should have anticipated what happened. Hadn't she noticed things changing in other areas of her life?

The way her parents' whispers came to a halt when she entered a room.

The way Yusef and his family were away from their home for prolonged periods, leaving their garden to wilt and die.

The way the headmaster could speak of little but new acquisitions for the school, though the pupils had yet to see any evidence of these purchases: tabla drums and tambourines, electric fans and lamps.

The way old women in the market would crescendo into hysteria as they spread rumours of daughters, sisters and wives being dishonoured before their families.

The way she'd overheard Ma say to Baba, *Should she go, ogo? Should she go?*

And his voice, almost a whisper: *Behave as though nothing has changed.*

Since things were changing elsewhere, perhaps it shouldn't have surprised Joya that something would be different when she entered Boromama's premises through the archway topped by two imposing red-eyed stone serpents, creatures Yusef had been terrified of when he'd visited the place.

She followed Maia through the lobby into the parlour, where the old man rose from his chair to greet his niece. He acknowledged the car driver with a nod. But when Joya crouched to touch Boromama's feet as a mark of respect, he shooed her away as if she were a stray dog. Joya remained crouching, stunned by his rejection. The old man seemed to mutter something under his breath, but she might have imagined it.

Maia's Boromama was usually friendly, sometimes overly so. Joya would often be relieved when the old man stopped pinching her cheeks or embracing her. She didn't like the way he peered at her nose through his thick-lensed spectacles. She disliked the way he cupped her chin and tilted her head back to look at her, even though she was almost as tall as he was. She despised the hot-rubber smell of his breath.

But this time, he'd pushed her aside as if she were a filthy rag.

'Come.' Maia pulled Joya towards the kitchen. 'Let's see if Mamima has ordered the cook to prepare nimbu paani for us.'

Maia's indifferent response to her uncle's rudeness made Joya wonder whether she herself had done something wrong. She was about to ask her friend what his behaviour meant, when the cook appeared.

'Here, take.' The woman passed Joya a glass of iced lemon water, which almost slipped from her fingers.

Perhaps Boromama had been distracted. After all, he was an eminent man, always busy. Or maybe there was a problem with his spectacles, and he hadn't realised who she was.

The afternoon humidity caused Joya's frock to stick to her skin. Once again, she considered asking her friend whether she'd done something to cause offence, but she wasn't sure how to broach the subject.

A maid brought a plate of pantua from Vikat's Emporium of Sweets, and Joya forgot the incident as she bit into a milky red-brown globe.

*

Maia took the first turn at the game that day.

'I used to drink milk from a boat-shaped bottle with a rubber teat.' That was believable. Joya had seen her cousin feeding from such a vessel until she was three years old.

She countered with a recollection about a visit to the police outpost where Baba was stationed. The head constable had allowed Joya to wear his hat.

The game progressed.

Maia told a tale about when she'd been in her mother's womb.

Joya shook her head.

'You think I'm fibbing?'

Joya nodded.

'Others recall past lives. Why would it be impossible for me to remember the beginning of this one?' Maia went on to describe the crosshatched marks on the walls of her mother's uterus, made by unborn siblings who'd perished before birth.

'How could you see?' Joya asked. 'Wasn't it dark in there?'

'Light penetrates from outside,' Maia said confidently. 'A reddish colour from the blood, like looking at the sun through closed eyelids.'

'I don't remember such a thing.'

Could Maia be right? Joya hadn't known about wombs and how babies grew until a few months earlier. There could be other things she didn't know.

Joya told Maia a story about meeting seven dwarfs in a wood.

'That's made up,' Maia interrupted. 'It's from a film. I saw it in the cinema. You even came with me, silly!'

'Caught me out,' Joya said. 'You win this round.'

'All right, here's one.' Maia dropped the last piece of pantua into her mouth, chewed thoughtfully, and then swallowed. 'When I was a baby, I overheard Mamima and Boromama talking.'

'What about?'

'Wait. Just listen.' Maia wiped her hands on a moistened gamcha the maid had placed in a brass basin. 'They were discussing how he had become so very rich.'

'But how did you understand? You were only a baby.'

'Shut up and listen. It was when I was an older baby, walking and talking.'

'So, it could have happened only last week?'

'Do you want to hear or not?' Maia pushed the pantua dish towards the maid who'd walked into the room.

'I'm listening,' Joya said. 'What did they say?'

Maia waited until the maid left. 'They said Boromama does people favours.'

'Favours?'

'Yah! And in return, they—' She sat up straight and stopped talking.

'More nimbu paani, girls?' Maia's aunt had crept into the room with a jug. 'What are you talking about?'

'Nothing, Mamima.'

Joya watched the swish of Maia's aunt's sari against the polished floor as she left the room. 'Go on. What did you hear next?'

'Nothing. I just made it up, all right? You win this round. Go on, it's your turn.'

Though it seemed there might have been more to Maia's story, Joya did as she was told, and took her turn. She recounted a trip with her father. 'I was three years old, riding on Baba's shoulders. He took me to see a magician.'

'A magician?' Maia's eyes widened.

'Yes,' Joya said, trying to sound important. 'He was dressed in black, had long hair and held a giant grasshopper in his hand.'

'How big was the grasshopper?'

'As big as the magician's hand.'

'Bhagavan! I've never seen such a large grasshopper.'

'Right before my eyes, the grasshopper turned into a frog.'

Maia's mouth opened. 'Then what?'

'The frog changed into a monkey.'

'No! How?' Maia could accept the transition between lower life forms, it seemed, but not frog to monkey. 'You're making this up.'

'He was a magician,' Joya continued. 'Very powerful.' She was losing herself in her own story. 'He could do anything.'

'Very well,' Maia said. 'What happened next?'

'The monkey passed a stool.'

'Ugh!'

'The stool was made of pure gold.'

'Oh! You should have stolen the monkey. Babaray! You could have made lakhs. You could have become rich.'

'What? And handle its poo? Its haga? The monkey's shit?' Joya grimaced. 'I wasn't touching that.'

'Not even for all those riches?'

'No. Would you?'

'If it was gold, then it *wouldn't* have been shit,' Maia said sourly.

'Well, what I did do was...'

Joya wove more and more improbable details into her story. It didn't matter that none of it was true. She wanted Maia to respect her, and those fantastic white lies were worth telling for that reason. When she realised Maia wasn't smiling anymore, she fell silent.

'It's true what they say about you,' Maia said with a leaden expression.

Joya realised she'd pushed the limits of her story too far. 'What?' she asked. 'Who says what?'

'You're just a fibber.'

'But...' Joya was confused. Wasn't that the whole point of the game? Weren't they supposed to weave in fantastical stories with the truth? She wondered if someone really had spoken about her, and what they'd said.

'And you people. Not content with what you have, you always want to take what rightfully belongs to others.'

'But—' Joya protested again.

'You prod and poke and you take, take, take.'

'Maia, has someone said something bad about me? I swear I haven't taken anything that wasn't freely given. What did they say? Who said it?'

'Oh.' Maia hesitated. 'It's nothing.'

'It can't be nothing,' Joya protested. 'Those things you said, they were—'

'Don't take it so seriously, yah?' Maia was smiling again.

'But what you said... What did you mean?'

'Array! It was only a joke,' Maia said, as if she was trying to erase everything that had passed in the last minute, as if the words had slipped from her mouth by accident. 'Don't you know a joke when you hear one?'

'It didn't sound like a joke,' Joya said.

'You people take life so seriously.'

Maia had never referred to Joya or her family as *you people* before. There had never been a feeling of *them and us* in their friendship.

'What do you mean?'

'Nothing. Come on, tell me more about this so-called magician,' Maia said.

But Joya found she had nothing more to say. Something was changing between them. Maia was no longer her closest friend, her confidante. She was changing into something else. Or maybe it was Joya who was different.

The Last Vacation

Sometimes they went north for the holidays. Joya's father loved hill stations with lush greenery and views of ice-capped mountains.

Her mother yearned for the clamour of the sea.

'May we go on a beach trip this time, ogo?' she had pleaded when they'd planned the vacation.

They took the train to Digha Sea Beach. Once they pulled out of Howrah, a heavy pall that had hung over the family dissipated. They ate paratha filled with potato and pomegranate seeds. Joya hadn't heard her parents laugh this way for months.

The family played 'ikri mikri chaam chikri' and other finger counting games, which Joya was far too old for at fourteen. Baba pretended a biting insect had landed on Ma's head, and tried to frighten her into slapping her own scalp. They joked about the man sharing their compartment. He spent most of the journey visiting the toilet.

'Babaray! Although I am enjoying the luxury of second-class travel compared to the hard benches in third,' Baba said, 'there is nothing enchanting about the WC facilities in these carriages.' He slapped his thigh. 'Why, he's been gone for over— Oh... pass me the tiffin carrier, Mamuni.' Joya's father rapidly changed the subject when the gentleman returned. Baba must have been in a light mood to address his wife by her pet name before a stranger. He turned to the man. 'May I offer you some light refreshment?'

The man accepted a paratha, joining his hands as if in prayer to offer thanks before taking the flatbread.

They reached their cabin at dusk, enjoying a scarlet sunset from their elevated position. Joya slept in a hammock on the veranda, shrouded by a voluminous mosquito net. Her parents' laughter continued long after they extinguished the lamp.

The cry of seabirds woke Joya at dawn. She couldn't remember where she was. Lifting her head to look for Ma caused the hammock to rock. Joya stepped down, and was alarmed to find the sea had disappeared. Everything swam in swirling mist.

'A sea fog.' Ma appeared behind her. 'Ah. I remember these from when I was a girl.'

'Did you come here often?'

'Here, Tajpur Beach and Shankarpur. Everywhere. I left part of my spirit by the sea.' Ma brushed her fingers through Joya's hair. 'Ish! So many knots. Why do you sleep with it untied? Let me comb.'

After the mist cleared, they walked on the waterfront barefoot.

'Why don't we step into the sea?' Joya asked.

'I'm not sure,' Baba said. 'It could be dangerous.'

'Not if we keep near the shore,' Ma said. 'And see over there?' She pointed to the nearby headland. 'My father used to say you should never go that far. Otherwise, it is safe.' She gathered her sari up and stepped in before any discussion could halt her. Joya followed. The water was tepid, like a pool of feathers around her feet. Baba entered the water, claimed it was too cold and headed back out. He was met by a large wave, which wet his dhuti up to the knees.

'See if you can find some shells,' Ma said when they came out. 'So I can decorate the house.'

'How shall I carry them?' Joya asked.

'Here.' Baba handed her his handkerchief. 'Use this.'

Joya pushed her bare toes through wet sand, revelling in the unfamiliar feeling. Most of the shells were triangular, white with purplish tips – cockles, she guessed. Some she knew to be painted ladies. The spiralling cornet-shaped ones were her favourite, though she didn't know their name.

She hummed a nursery rhyme Master-Moshai had taught her years ago.

Mary, Mary, quite contrary
How does your garden grow?

She thought about her mother's friend Mary D'Costa with her long, hooked nose. Mary was a happy woman. Especially since she had divorced that rogue of a husband, Christopher.

'Mary, Mary' wasn't a happy song, her teacher had explained. Some said it was about a British queen who tortured and executed people who held different beliefs.

With silver bells and cockle shells
And pretty maids all in a row.

Master-Moshai had told them *silver bells* were instruments of torture, designed to crush a person's fingers or toes. But as Joya hummed to herself on the beach, she felt far removed from cruelty and danger. She wondered whether her friend Maia had ever been on a holiday like this. Maia's family had servants and a motorcar, and would soon have a telephone: wealth Joya's family would never see. And yet, could those luxuries bring as much happiness as the sound of the sea and a handful of God's creations? She wished Maia could share the beauty with her.

Walking back to her parents, Joya cut through a stand of narrow trees. Dead leaves and pebbles pricked her feet. The shells felt cool in her father's handkerchief.

Ma and Baba were sitting near the water's edge, both soaked above chest height. Their hair glistened with seawater. Had they ventured further into the waves despite her father's reservations? An occasional word floated towards her. Joya stopped walking. Her father sounded apprehensive.

'…there is a cost to integrity.'

Joya wondered what they were talking about.

'What cost?' Ma asked, alarmed.

'Mamuni, I…' Rustling leaves obscured some words. '…an empty threat.'

'Babaray! The snake and his goondas…'

Joya took a step closer. Perhaps she would discover what was causing the tension she'd sensed for months.

'He is a very cunning man.'

'How sure are you that it's him?'

'Mamuni, we can't be a hundred per cent certain, otherwise our work would be so much simpler.'

'It frightens me. He's never far from us, ogo. He could—'

'I've been thinking. Should we move her from that school?'

'But she loves it. Her friends attend, and there are boys from good families who might make a good husband.'

'Array! There is time enough to think of husbands!'

'It's that śayatāna headmaster, isn't it? The devil on our doorstep. He is involved too, isn't he?'

'We shouldn't speak openly of these things. One never knows who might hear.'

Ma turned to look around. The line of her mouth curved slightly. She stood to greet her daughter.

'Come,' she said. 'There's a man selling jalebi from a cart.'

'He can't have gone far,' Baba added. 'Let's find him.'

Both were smiling, but Joya knew those smiles were painted over fear.

Exodus

Joya finds it hard to remember people's smiles when they've gone – their smiles and their eyes.

She looks at the mirror in the bathroom. Her irises are pale brown, like the tail feathers of a house sparrow. There are corn-coloured flecks towards the periphery. Though the mirror is frosty and the silvering has browned, peeling away in places, the image of her eyes is clearer than the memory of Yusef's.

Yusef was the nearest thing she had to a brother. They'd played together since they were babies, their mothers close as sisters. Maybe he was more than a brother to her. But he isn't here anymore.

Faarooq Uncle's family had been away so often in the past year that Joya hadn't realised they'd gone, actually gone, until the day she peered through a dusty window to discover the neighbours had vanished for good.

They hadn't taken everything.

The beds still had balled-up eiderdowns half on, half pouring onto the floor at the footboard. The almaris gaped like open mouths, revealing gaps where perhaps a winter coat or shawl might have hung once. It was easier to see what had been left than to remember what was missing: tattered kurtas covered in patches suspended on lopsided hangers; faded saris with frayed borders; odd socks; a woollen glove unravelling at the fingertips.

There was enough missing for Joya to know the family wouldn't come back.

Joya looks in the mirror again, and wipes her tears away with her sleeve.

Gone, of Course

'Why did they leave without saying goodbye?'
she'd demanded when Baba had returned from the
police station the evening she realised Yusef had
gone for good.

But soon after, Baba himself was gone.

Joya was lying in bed the day Baba disappeared. She
was enjoying the ashen smell of rooti cooking on the
coal brazier. That scent was the only call needed to
wake her.

She didn't need a sunrise bugler blasting
a reveille, although the cadets from a distant
barracks could be heard when the wind blew in a
certain direction.

She didn't need a ticking alarm clock with
poisonous luminous dials, although one stood silent
on the mantelpiece. Dadu, her grandfather, had passed
the piece to Joya's mother because his daughter had

admired the clock, even though its mechanism had failed a decade before Joya was born.

She didn't need a moistened gamcha brought by a servant, sweet with lavender oil, although for Maia that was the only way to be woken for school.

Shorbonaash!

Ma spoke of the destruction of all things – a term that had come to be used lightly for everyday situations such as when the milk boiled over, when a mynah bird shat on drying laundry or when Joya risked being late for school, because she'd dawdled over her rooti and egg at breakfast. But the thunderous way her mother said the word, followed by her wails and stifled moans, suggested this was different. The word was followed by Ma's cries, like a torn rag, saying over and over again, 'Don't go, ogo, don't leave us.'

And then silence.

Joya didn't dare step out of her room. The savoury aroma of breakfast dissipated soon after the first *shorbonaash*. Her hunger curdled into a solid lump at the base of her belly.

Eventually, curiosity forced her out of her room. The coals appeared still and grey until she poked them to release a shower of sparks.

Six rooti lay on a platter on the table underneath a beaded cloth. The bread was flat and cold. The aloo bhaja Ma had made sat in a covered glass dish. Normally, Joya would have prised the lid open and popped a piece of spiced potato into her mouth, but all she wanted to do that morning was find her parents.

Joya found her mother in the garden. She asked where her father was, and all Ma said was, 'Why? He's gone, of course,' as if the catastrophe Joya had heard earlier had never happened.

Perhaps it had only been milk for Baba's coffee boiling over.

Yet in the hours, days and weeks that followed, there was no sign of Baba. He hadn't taken anything from the closets. His tongue scraper and shaving brush sat on the shelf at the base of the mirror. His razor gathered dust and started to rust.

The new shirt Ma had made him for Durga Puja, neatly pressed, hung in the almari. His gamcha hung over a peg on the bathroom door. The cloth had dried to a crisp. His cup sat unused in the cupboard. A sprinkling of red dust had covered it.

It didn't take long for things to change after someone left.

The Last Day

That Tuesday, not long after Durga Puja, began innocently enough.

In the morning, Maia caught Joya on the pathway in front of the school hall.

'What are you doing after school?' she asked.

Joya was thinking about her lunch: two rooti rolled into cigar shapes packed in the stainless-steel tiffin carrier inside her school bag. The flatbread contained spiced potatoes her mother had fried that morning.

'Nothing.'

'There's a badminton tournament.' Maia named children who like herself lived in the wealthy compound near the site where the new school building was to be built – the new school where the fabled tabla drums, tambourines, fans and lamps might eventually appear. 'You should come.'

'I don't know. I have so much studying, yah?'

'*He* might come.'

Maia's secret relationship with her poet had intensified after they'd begun meeting in person. To date, they had avoided being discovered by anyone who might report them to her parents. But if Michael was to be at the tournament, Joya thought it even more important she should *not* be there. Instead of decreasing, his letters were arriving more frequently, as he and Maia arranged and rearranged times and places to meet. Ma was becoming suspicious about the brown envelopes that came addressed to Joya.

'Why so many letters?' Ma had asked a few days earlier. 'Who is sending?' Her mother had become increasingly jittery and nervous in the days since Baba had gone away, always evasive when Joya asked when he would return. Ma was becoming more protective towards her too. Joya thought she might have to ask Maia to find someone else to receive Michael's correspondence.

'I'd better not,' she told her friend. 'So much studying.'

The mathematics teacher was writing an equation on the board when the headmaster came in and called Joya to his office. She wondered if he was going to reprimand her. Perhaps her role in Maia's illicit love affair had been discovered. But why had Maia herself not been summoned? Joya followed the grey-haired man along the corridor. Her heart rate quickened.

'Sit down,' he told her, not unkindly, once they were in the office.

Joya sat at the desk and folded her hands. The master's cringing smile reassured her, but only a little. Maybe it was something good after all. Perhaps she had been nominated for a prize or scholarship. Ma and Baba found enough for school fees, but the cost of books and other equipment was sometimes hard to meet. And now Baba had disappeared and her mother wouldn't tell her where or for how long, how would they even manage the fees?

'Miss Guho.' The head often used formal titles for serious matters. Joya tried not to raise her hopes. 'There have been some…' He hesitated, as if searching for the best words. 'There have been changes, and it is with deep regret that I must ask you to leave this institution.'

Joya listened in silence, though she wanted to ask many questions.

For how long do I have to leave?

What have I done?

The headmaster continued, as thoughts whirled through her mind:

Is my family no longer considered good enough?

Were my grades incorrect all these years?

Have I done something to disgrace the school's name?

The headmaster kept speaking, but nothing he said answered Joya's questions. She had no idea why she'd been singled out. Cast away. Expelled! Shame gnawed at her belly like a parasite. And yet – and yet, could this be linked with events in her home life? Joya couldn't make a connection, and yet a shadowy memory about the headmaster surfaced. Something she'd overheard before their lives had somersaulted into chaos.

Should we move her from that school?

It's that śaÿatāna headmaster, isn't it? He is involved too, isn't he?

The man was still speaking, his voice obsequious, tinny and devoid of meaning.

He said someone had been dispatched to collect her school bag. Joya must leave the premises immediately and never return. Unexpectedly, she found herself wondering whether the stuffed rooti would still be in the bag when it arrived.

It was easier to fixate on tangible issues. Everything else was too big.

Unfathomable.

Morning Call

Baba had always insisted Joya receive a good education. So why wasn't she at school anymore? And if not *that* school, which other would she enrol in?

She marched towards the compound. The rosewood trees swayed in the breeze. The smallest one, whose low branches she and Yusef used to climb when they were little, reminded Joya her friend was gone too, the half-completed cricket bat left on the hardened earth at the back of the compound.

The weight of her school bag was all she could feel.

She couldn't detect the hum of the earth beneath her feet.

She couldn't hear the buzz of insects that flew around her school hat and alighted on her skin.

She couldn't smell the autumnal earth scents that rose from ditches surrounding the fields she passed on her way home.

Nothing was the same.

*

Joya wondered what she would find when she arrived home. She unlocked the door to find Ma sitting at the table wearing a white sari over a long, plain chemise. Ma didn't own a white sari. There was a delicate cream silk with violet flowers embroidered on the border, a white shawl with grey bird shapes incorporated into part of the weave, but no white sari. The cloth wasn't new. There were worn patches and scuff marks around the lower edge. Had Ma bought it from the market stall that sold tattered rags people were throwing out?

'Tell me what's happening,' Joya demanded.

'Nothing is happening,' Ma replied. Her face was drawn, yet puffy around the eyes, as if she had been crying. Why hadn't she asked why Joya was home early? Why hadn't she asked whether she was sick, or if she'd misbehaved in class?

'I was asked to leave school.'

'Perhaps it's better this way.' Ma took a potato from the pile in the bowl in front of her and peeled it with a paring knife.

'Did you know this would happen?' Joya pulled a chair out and sat opposite her mother.

'I didn't think he would do it.'

'Do what? Who?'

'No matter. We have to decide what to do next.'

'There's another school not far from here. We can try there.'

'The one where children of servants go?'

'Does it matter who goes? School is school.' Joya felt increasingly annoyed at her mother, even though it wasn't Ma who had kicked their life into chaos.

'Do you think you can learn your calculus and big ideas in such a school?'

'At least I will learn something.' Joya was hot. She wanted to tear her school uniform off as she normally did upon returning home. But it occurred to her that once she took it off, she might never wear it again.

'Where is Baba?' she asked. 'Why isn't he back yet?'

'Baba isn't coming back.'

'Doesn't he... doesn't he want us anymore?' Joya remembered Ma's friend Mary D'Costa, who had been relieved when she and Christopher divorced. But Ma and Baba weren't like that. And why was Ma dressed like a widow?

'He can never return.'

'But why?'

'Joya, you're not a baby anymore. Try to understand.'

'Understand what? Tell me!'

'I *am* telling.'

'But where is he?'

'Joya, your father is gone. Bhagavan will take care of him.'

Neither of them said anything. There was nothing to break the silence. The clock on the mantelpiece was mute, as always. Realisation dripped like water. It covered the walls, saturated the windows, percolated through Joya's ears, fell around her feet and sank into the earth. If her father was with God, why, that surely meant... She didn't scream. She didn't wail. She didn't even ask how it had happened.

'If he's dead, why have we not...' And that was when the tears came, blurring her vision. 'If he's dead, where did his body go?'

All Ma said in reply was, 'I am sending you to stay with Tiya Mashi until I find some solutions to our problems.'

'Tiya Mashi's? What problems? Aren't you coming? And how long will I be gone for?'

'A few weeks. Maybe less. Maybe more.'

AT TIYA
MASHI'S HOUSE

Mother's Love

Ma sent Joya away to a village on the edge of a mining town.

She didn't weep. She didn't warn her daughter about dangers she might face on the road: overzealous hawkers, dacoits, lepers and thieves, potholes, deluges and mudslides. Snakes. She didn't press a coin into her daughter's palm for luck, as Joya had come to expect before a long journey. Ma didn't fill the tiffin carrier with sweetmeats, as she usually did for rail trips.

Ma didn't warn her about rising tensions between different groups that should have been on the same side. Joya's mother wasn't like Rukhsana Khala. Joya had once heard her old neighbour tell her son how factions within the same religion opposed one another's ideas as zealously as those who worshipped different deities. She remembered Yusef listening quietly with wide eyes, while she kicked a ball on the hard earth behind their house, hoping he'd join her in play soon.

Ma hadn't accepted Joya's pronaam before she stepped into the rickshaw, instead pulling her daughter up by the arm when she bent to touch her mother's sandalled feet.

Ma didn't want a fuss.

The tight knots in Ma's face might have been grief, but her sorrow was barely visible, a plain non-smile ironed over her skin. She'd wrapped the pallu of her white sari around her hibiscus-oiled locks, so Joya could neither touch nor see her mother's soft hair before she went.

Joya waved.

Her mother didn't wave back. Perhaps she didn't want to attract the attention of the snake that had killed Joya's father. Was Baba really dead? Ma had told her so, and yet she had never used the words.

Words.

Joya remembered her mother's words: *You know best, ogo.* Ma had acquiesced when Joya's father insisted their daughter receive a good education.

Her mother wasn't a woman who told lies.

Joya craned her neck as the rickshaw pulled away towards the train station.

Ma looked towards a distant horizon.

*

When she is sent to Tiya Mashi's house, Joya worries her heels in the blue dust that gets into everything. She rides on the back of a scooter with her cousin

Aroti, the sharp tang of gasoline from the engine casing invading her nostrils as they soar past fields of flowers that grow without reason; no helmets, because the helmets in the house are for Aroti's brothers and for Mesho-Moshai, because Aroti's father is indispensable.

When she is sent away, Joya and her cousins stay out far later than they are allowed, playing floodlit badminton, ignoring the Noamundi boys who come to the village and hover like flies waiting for a flash of a knee or accidental touch of skin. The odour of the place stays in her nose like stale snot. The stench of the long-drop toilet competes with the red smell from the steelworks in the distance.

When she is sent away, Joya tries not to hear sympathetic whispers that flow under the gap of her uncle and aunt's door, Mesho-Moshai's voice soaring higher and loftier than Tiya Mashi's, her aunt's voice soft like a caged bird's, her uncle's soprano tone leaden with piety.

When she is sent away, Joya peers at the sky through a gap in the curtains, tries not to cry, so her cousins won't discover that despite their efforts she struggles to keep the weight of sorrow behind her eyes.

When she is sent away, Joya lies in the wide-wide bed shared with Aroti and the other girl cousins in a confusion of smells: apples and gasoline. She twirls feathers she has pulled from the fine weave of her pillow around her index finger, imagines they are strands of her mother's hair.

*

Later, they will rarely speak of Joya's period of exile.

Later, when Joya performs tasks previously done by her father, she won't ask why the duties fall to her. Later, after Joya has wired a Bakelite plug, cracked the skull of a coconut or paid the doodwallah for the milk, she won't ask her mother again why she sent her away, because her questions will again likely be met by words that elicit more questions.

Instead she will dream of lying in her mother's bed, knotting her fingers through Ma's hair and slipping a thumb into her mouth as she did when she was a little girl.

In Exile

Joya imagined herself to be one of seven dwarfs from the story she'd heard as a child. Like the dwarfs she and her girl cousins were stacked up in one bed. She couldn't remember whether her memory of the dwarfs' sleeping arrangements was from reading the original story, or the film Maia's parents had taken a group of her friends to see at the cinema on her birthday.

If she and her younger cousins were dwarfs, then Aroti Didi, the eldest, was Snow White. With her fairer skin, her penchant for apples, poisoned or not, the magic she worked around her eyes in front of the mirror with kajol, her rides on smoke-sputtering motorbikes, and the occasional stolen biri that left different fumes about her person after she smoked. Their didi was an unlikely heroine, but no one else filled the role's dimensions.

Had the Brothers Grimm travelled a century into their future and come to the yellow-skied steel town in semi-rural India where Joya was held captive, they could perhaps have created a story for her; maybe a play.

Joya imagined actors rehearsing on the stage of the new school that was being built in her hometown. Perhaps she would be cast as a dwarf. Or maybe an elf. Elves were hard-working creatures who helped others to benefit from their industry. Perhaps Joya-elf could manufacture something, something for Baba – some shoes. Or a coat? A suit?

For in this play, Baba would be sure to return.

When their family catastrophe was over, the players would laugh about how Joya, one of their own, had been sent away and eventually returned safely.

Naturally, Tiya Mashi would have a role in Joya's story. But how would her aunt be written? A mother-substitute, who was complicit in the plot? She kept Joya in a town where you could taste metal from the air seeping into your gums. Joya's aunt couldn't be a fairy godmother. She was merely a fiery one. She was no saviour.

Joya was angry with her aunt for blackening her eyes with kajol and lies, but she didn't want Tiya Mashi to dance herself to death in a pair of red-hot iron slippers, as in the Grimm story. After all, her mother, too, had revealed that her father was dead, without actually *telling* her that Baba had died.

And Mesho-Moshai? Who would he be in the play? For her jolly uncle, smoking biris on the sly so his wife suspected him only because of the smell he denied, was no gruff woodsman. Neither was he king or prince.

None of the characters suited their parts well.

There were heroes and villains in Joya's story, as in any other, the latter as determined to destroy their enemies as any wicked stepmother. Perhaps it was the snake in all his guises? Only Joya didn't know how the two-tailed snake would be portrayed. She didn't know who he was, though she had heard enough whisperings to surmise he had a role in Baba's fate.

If the Brothers Grimm *could* come to her, if they held magical powers and influence that came with it, Joya wouldn't ask them to write her a fairy tale. Instead, she'd ask for a happy ending in real life. If anyone could rewrite the future, Joya would ask that she return home to Baba and her mother, whose crooked-toothed smile she missed so much her own teeth hurt.

Cousins

Priya is Joya's youngest cousin. Aroti is the oldest of the girls. Priya is prone to tears and screaming. Aroti likes apples. She also smokes and drinks behind her parents' backs, and is proud of her pale-pale skin, almost like paper.

Joya herself is dark like her mother, tall like her father. She has inherited Ma's glassy eyes. She has trouble remembering what her father's eyes are like. It will come to her in time.

All her cousins have dark brown eyes that they describe as black.

My eyes are black.

There are boy cousins too, but Joya finds it hard to keep track of them, with their small moustaches, black eyes (sometimes from fighting) and bad teeth. They look similar and behave in the same manner as one another. The boys are all older than the girls, just like Maia's boy cousins are, but these boys don't smell of overripe fruit and burning as Maia's do.

The boy cousins keep a respectable distance from Joya. This is not out of respect for her, she fears, but rather because they fear they'll catch the miasma of her bad fortune if they come too close. They go about their business as if they live in another layer of the house; their path only intersects with others' at mealtimes.

Joya has only one source of cousins, her mother's sister. She's been told Baba had no brothers or sisters. It's hard to know how much is true, and how much is lies when your world has been turned upside down. Had. Has. Had.

She's surmised Baba's family were not pleased with his choice of bride. It's hard to imagine anyone disapproving of Ma, with her complicated smile and soft hair. But there are other factors involved when deciding whether a girl is a good match.

It's hard to think of Baba as the unmarried boy he once was.

Joya wonders what it would have been like to meet her parents before they'd met one another. She knows such a thing is impossible, but wonders whether the three of them could have been friends. They might have formed a triangle. Baba from his tribe, Ma from hers, and Joya from a tribe of her own formed by the two of theirs.

Her cousins are purebred. They teach her to ride a bicycle.

Mesho-Moshai, her burly uncle, is fifteen years older than Tiya Mashi. He has never forgiven Baba for his parents' disapproval. *Who do they think they are? What do they have that makes them better than we are?* Even if he doesn't ever utter those words in front of Joya, his distaste seeps from his body through the pores in his skin, leaving her wondering how a matchmaker could have paired Ma and Baba in the first instance.

Joya's aunt was fourteen, the same age as Joya is, when she married. Joya's grandparents, Dadu and Dida, bred Tiya into Mesho-Moshai's family. Their union is said to be a good match. The oldest boy cousin, Something-or-Other Dada, was born less than a year after the wedding, Joya has been told. She relies on what she's been told for events that happened before her birth. Baba wasn't even in the same family when Something-or-Other Dada was born, although they were still Joya's family then, though she hadn't yet been born.

She depends on others to understand events that take place now, though half of what she's told may be lies. It would be easier if they lied about everything, and then she'd know to believe the exact opposite.

So many people are coming and going, some head east, others west, as determined by the colour of their gods. Some, swept along like flotsam, have lost everything. Those who remain on the wrong side of boundaries that don't yet exist will be forced to move. That's what people say. Joya is marooned in this place, near Noamundi towards the west, where Aroti smears kajol around her eyes and goes riding on her brother's motorbike to meet unsuitable friends. Everyone knows about this apart from Mesho-Moshai and Tiya Mashi, who would skin their daughter alive if they discovered she wasn't in the library studying as she said.

Shanti is three years younger than Joya. The eleven-year-old is quietly spoken. She is tall for her age, but not nearly as tall as Joya.

Joya's aunt, uncle and cousins aren't the only people to be found in the house near Noamundi. There is an old lady called Neha who keeps everyone under control. She holds a detailed timetable in her head and knows where everyone should be at any time, even those who plan to be somewhere they are not supposed to be. Ostensibly, she is the family's cook, but Neha's responsibilities extend far beyond the kitchen. Priya calls her Neha Didu, as if she is a surrogate grandmother in the absence of real ones.

Chondon, the driver, is secretly in love with Aroti, but this is the worst-kept secret in the whole household. He doesn't live on the premises as Neha does. It wouldn't be considered proper, even more so since Neha found little square studio photographs of Aroti in his jacket pocket when he'd secreted his outerwear into the laundry pile in the hope of having it washed for free. Of course no one but Neha knows about the find, except that everyone does. Everyone except Mesho-Moshai and Tiya Mashi, who would skin *him* alive if they found out, and that can't be allowed to happen. It's not easy to find drivers this far from Noamundi.

Behind Tiya
Mashi's House

Neha asked the girls to venture to the plot behind the house.

Joya remembered Mesho-Moshai had once said it was dangerous there.

'Snakes and other abominable creatures,' her uncle had warned.

The snake, Joya thought. *How far can he reach? Isn't that why Ma sent me here?*

She wondered why the cook wanted them to go into forbidden territory.

'There's a saucepan I want you to fetch,' Neha said.

'Whose saucepan?' Aroti demanded. As the eldest, she was in charge.

'It belongs to your mother. She needs it back,' Neha snapped. She was crouching at a boti, making light work of chopping taro with the suicidal blade that projected from the base of the implement she used to cut everything from tiny fish to coconuts.

Joya had never heard Neha speak that way to her aunt or uncle. It was all *no please, yes thank you* when she spoke with the heads of the household. But Neha found courage when talking to the youngsters who had transitioned from babes with wet bottoms to young women under her watch.

Joya followed the line of girl cousins, single file behind Aroti. As they walked into the tiny concrete yard, a place where stray cats came to piss, the littlest girl turned to ask the kitchen hand a question.

'How did the pan get there, Neha Didu?' Priya's voice was always either a cry or a question.

'Choop!' Neha shouted, holding a large taro up like a club. 'So many questions from such a small mouth.'

'How are we going to find anything?' Aroti asked. 'There's so much rubbish.'

There were twisted tin cans, old bones and ruptured mattresses, feathers escaping from the seams. Books with pages torn out, rags and unidentifiable masses of yellowish foam.

'Why do people throw everything here?' Joya asked, but knew as the question left her mouth that she needn't have asked it, for this was where Neha herself discarded everything from fish heads to blood-stained rags that refused to wash clean.

'We don't even know which of Ma's bloody saucepans we're supposed to find,' Aroti said. 'And I'm going to a function soon.'

'Didi, I'm scared.' Priya clutched Aroti's leg.

'What's to be scared of, little monkey?' her sister asked. 'Only a few snakes, including a python Chondon said he saw here last week.'

Priya screamed.

Joya lifted the girl into her arms. 'A python? Really?' Joya was a little concerned at the prospect of such a large snake.

'Ha,' Aroti said. 'If that bhitoo cowardy-cat thought it was a python, it was probably only an earthworm.' She tossed her hair back in a dismissive gesture.

'Earthworms, I can manage,' Shanti said, 'but I'd heard there might be a rakkhosh somewhere out here.'

Joya felt Priya squirm as the child swiped tears from her eyes with her fists.

'And I heard the rakkhosh likes the taste of little girls,' Shanti continued.

Priya screamed again.

'Is this the one?' Shanti held a dented steel pan with no handle.

'That's it,' Aroti said, 'though who knows how it got this far from the house.'

The girls returned the pan to its rightful place. Neha barely acknowledged their labour, instead dismissing them from the kitchen with a wave.

Joya was fascinated as she watched her cousin dress, undress and re-dress before heading to the community hall. Even though she was pushed for time, Aroti tried on almost every item in her wardrobe. She wasn't performing in the bharatnatyam dance as some of her classmates were, but it was clearly critically important that she dressed spectacularly for the occasion, with not a trace of evidence that she had been scrabbling about in a rubbish heap less than an hour earlier.

A Waste of Tears

They saw a car speeding away. Momentarily silenced as a crowd gathered around a prostrate form ahead, Joya and Aroti kept walking.

It's rude to stare.

Joya remembered something her mother often said.

Look away.

Joya's father used to tease Ma about her pieces of wisdom.

'What? You are a Britisher now, Mamuni? Must we not look at others?'

Ma's face had turned aubergine.

'Nah, ogo,' she'd replied, pulling her kapoor over her face, as if she needed to hide her teeth because they didn't fit properly. 'Just something I learned.' Ma would never specify whom she'd learned these *just somethings* from.

'Next you'll be eating with knife-spoon and wiping your bottom with a handkerchief,' Baba had

said. They'd all laughed. He'd laughed so hard the
flesh on his cheeks had wobbled.

Joya turned back to look at the body. Aroti stopped
and did the same, drawn towards something they
desperately didn't want to see.

The boy's legs were twitching.

'Only nerve activity,' Aroti said. 'Look away.'

At breakfast, Joya's father ate moglai paratha with a
knife and fork. He praised Ma, chewing on a piece.
'Perfect. Neither too hard nor too soft. Daroon hoychay!
Truly brilliant.' For everything else, he used his fingers.

Aroti pulled Joya's arm. 'Come on.'

The crowd around the boy had grown.

'Should we help?' Joya asked her cousin as they
retreated. The boy couldn't have been more than
sixteen. Maybe he was younger. Perhaps only fourteen
as Joya was. She'd noticed a hint of a moustache on
his upper lip, along with the crimson of his freshly
spilled blood.

The twitching had stopped.

'Nooooo!' Aroti had replied. 'His people are
there. They will take care of it. They won't want
everybody staring.' The older girl pulled her dupatta
tight around herself, as if warding off a spirit that
had been liberated. 'Ish! The poor mother.'

Was it rude to walk away? There was little they could do, Joya thought. Perhaps pay their respects or offer a description of the beige car that had fled after rolling over the boy.

'How would you have felt, Didi,' Joya asked, 'if it was one of your brothers and people walked away as if he were a dead dog, nothing more?'

'Don't ask stupid questions,' Aroti replied. 'I wouldn't want people to stand around like chickens, beaks opening and closing.'

Joya remembered walking with Ma through the fields near where they lived. The monsoon wet had caused silver mushrooms to appear overnight.

Joya had bent to pick one.

'Nooooo!' Ma had shouted. 'Chi chi chi.' Scolding Joya as if she were a tiny child. 'Don't you know they are poison?'

Joya and Aroti were halfway home when the tears came.

'Bhagavan!' Aroti invoked God's name, tugging her cousin's sleeve. 'You cannot cry over such things.'

'Why not?' Joya had yelled. She wanted to stamp her foot. A boy was dead, albeit a stranger, one of hundreds who died on the roads daily in India. And yet Joya couldn't stop thinking about him. Had he known his fate?

'You have far more to cry about, sister. Don't waste tears on such things.'

Aroti's words made Joya cry harder.

She had tears enough.

She'd cry about Baba whom she'd not said goodbye to. Baba who was gone, and yet not gone, like a sadhu who must declare himself dead in the eyes of the law before leaving to learn the scriptures from his guru. Some even attended their own funerals, she had heard.

Joya had tears enough to cry for her absent mother.

And she had tears enough for the boy.

The boy who had no idea when he woke up in the morning that this would be the last day of his life.

The Journey

When Ma arrived to take Joya home, she had tears enough for both of them.

Joya took her mother's hands and washed dust from them with wet kisses.

'Why did you take so long?' she asked. 'Couldn't you have come earlier?'

'Let her rest.' Tiya Mashi untangled mother and daughter. 'You're not a baby, Joya. I was already married when I was fourteen.'

'I haven't seen Ma for so long,' Joya pleaded.

'Aroti!' her aunt cried. 'Take your cousin-sister.'

Joya turned back to look at her mother as she was led away. She was struck by how shrunken her mother looked in a ghost-pale sari, a luminous quality about her. And her eyes! The fear in them frightened Joya. It seemed Ma had cried her eyes red. They reminded Joya of the Kathakali dancers she had seen long ago, touring from the south. They wore thick green make-up, tall headpieces and wide skirts. The whites of their eyes were a fiery colour. Baba had told her they reddened their eyes by inserting a Chundappoo seed into the lower lid – they kept it there for the duration of the performance. The idea had made her shudder. Why deliberately redden the eyes? Red eyes. Red stones. The stone serpents that guarded Maia's uncle's house had red stone eyes. Those snakes had terrified Yusef. Yet other snakes were far more destructive than the inert reptiles at Boromama's house.

Lost in her thoughts, Joya followed Aroti to the place where they slept. The room was almost entirely occupied by the bed. There was little space to manoeuvre even their slim bodies. The girls clambered onto the elephant-print bedspread to play cards. The patterned counterpane reminded Joya of a wall hanging in Maia's house. But Maia was far away, and only Bhagavan knew when she'd see her friend again.

Aroti was squabbling with her younger sisters. They argued about who deserved to be dealt the black queen, the Bibi. Priya shuffled the cards. She might have been young but, like the others, the girl was aware the two black queens were not equal.

Ishkapon or Chiraton?

Spades or clubs?

The Ishkapon queen spelled disaster.

'Don't look at them,' Aroti said, biting into a green apple. 'Why shuffling so slowly, kid?'

The little girl hesitated, cards threatening to slip from her fingers.

'I can't do it faster, Didi,' she pleaded.

'Here. Let me.' Shanti took the pack, though it wasn't her turn to deal. 'Where is the Ishkapon Bibi?' she chanted. 'Whose lap will she fall into?'

Even before the cards left her cousin's fingers, Joya knew she had been dealt the most difficult hand, because cards alone didn't determine those things.

She listened for her mother, heard the thump of feet on stairs, her uncle's sonorous voice.

A door slammed. Joya looked back at her hand, discovered it was her turn. Aroti wobbled her head, but Joya couldn't decipher whether her older cousin's gesture implied approval or dismay.

Later, when she went to the outhouse to relieve herself, Joya heard raised voices from an open window upstairs.

'Why you told her this?' Tiya Mashi sounded sad.

'Babaray! I had to say something,' Ma said. 'She's always asking, asking, asking!'

Joya wondered who the *she* her mother referred to was. Could they be speaking about her?

'We've tried to protect her,' Mesho-Moshai boomed. 'So terrible for the child.'

Ma said, 'Better she sees what everyone sees. Young tongues—'

But then the sound of Shanti and Priya chasing each other through the courtyard obliterated any further words from above.

The next morning, a sulphurous smell from the steelworks stained Joya's dream yellow, and pulled her back into the reality she'd been avoiding.

She'd dreamed about Baba again. Her father was godlike in the vision, with blue skin and extra eyes he hadn't possessed in the real world. But before she could speak to him, Baba had left, his white dhuti-Punjabi flowing behind him.

Priya and the other girls filled the air with morning cries.

The house was alive with activity.

Has Neha warmed the water?

Where's my green kurta?

Who's tidied the shoes? Where are my chappals?

'There is some delay,' Tiya Mashi said, flipping a paratha in the pan. 'Chondon needs a new tyre for the car. Neha! Have you packed Joya's tiffin carrier?'

Neha wound between family members, moving this and that, wiping, washing, helping to keep her charges clean and fed. She'd worked with the family long enough to anticipate what they needed, often before they knew it themselves.

On the way to the station, Joya opened the lunch Neha had packed. She passed a luchi filled with spiced potatoes to her mother, and offered one to Chondon. But he said he never ate while driving.

They'd be on the train in less than an hour. It would take several more to reach Howrah. Ma sat in silence, her white sari wrapped around her like a shroud. Joya looked forward to the rickshaw ride from the station to their tiny house, with little idea of what lay ahead in days to come. She felt it unwise to mention Baba while Chondon was in the driver's seat whistling a tune from a movie through his teeth. She wouldn't ask about school either, but would wait until Ma let her know where she'd enrolled her. What about the lessons she'd missed in the weeks she'd been away, though? And was the danger that had befallen her father a threat to her mother and herself? No one would tell her what had happened, and she sensed that there were things she shouldn't ask about, as if uttering them might tempt fate to curse their lives.

There was much uncertainty: what had happened to Baba, how her education would progress, where the people who'd left the city had fled to, and if there was still a possibility the two-tailed snake might harm them.

However, one thing was certain. There was one more stuffed luchi for the journey ahead than there might otherwise have been.

AFTER EVERYTHING CHANGES

Snakes II

Array bhai!

You believe we are all evil? Are we fanged creatures only capable of inflicting pain and suffering? Some of us are good. Some are gods – you know that, of course. You have heard of Ananta, surely, to name but one? You know these things, as you know some gods have less good intent than others.

But let's speak of *good*.

Take a moment to consider the good we do for the world. Shall I make a list?

No, I see you're not in the mood to listen.

It is one serpent in particular you dread, isn't that so? The two-tailed snake!

I've told you before, I am indifferent to matters pertaining to good or evil, whether they relate to the dalliances of *Homo sapiens* or anguine matters. I am an impartial observer, if you like.

But what is it about this man? Or is he a snake, or a statue? Or is he two snakes? Or a man? Or a snake? Or a man-snake?

Call me brazen. I'm not scared to utter his name. Why, some call him B—

But I can't give him away yet. Not when there is so much more to tell.

Don't sit there like a statue yourself. Come. Let's make a list of what he has done. You don't want to know about the good, but you are *so* concerned about the bad. *Bad, bad, bad, bad, bad.* What does that say about you?

He has:

- Taken bribes. So what? Doesn't everybody?
- Perverted the course of justice. *Tut tut tut!* I am but a common snake. I don't pretend to understand the vagaries of how *Iustitia* operates – such a fickle lady is she.
- Diverted funds meant for the benefit of all into his own scaly pocket. Some say he is merely being rewarded for his cunning.
- Beaten his adversaries and buried their bones where no one will ever find them. I would challenge that. His kitten-soft hands have never struck a person in anger. (He doesn't need to. He has plenty who will do his bidding.)

- Moved money from here to there, from there to here and back again, until the slimy trail grows cold and untraceable. Isn't there a name for that profession? Isn't it the second oldest profession in the world? Don't bhadralok send their sons to university to learn how to do just that? *Ah*, you cry. *It's different when* gentlemen *do it*. And yet isn't the two-tailed snake the gentlest of them all?

I see your attention is wavering. The snake has friends in high places. And low ones. How easily I can divert you with my sleight of tail. Ha ha! So easy.

What about you? I hear your question.

Me?

I am but a simple snake. Sometimes I wear a turban. Sometimes I wear a top hat. Sometimes I wear nothing at all on my head, but slither into the undergrowth where you'll struggle to find me.

Farewell!

Calculations

Joya took the tiffin carrier from her mother and tucked it into her rucksack. The warmth seeped through the canvas and reached her back, for there were no books or gym paraphernalia within to redistribute the heat from the rice and ghee balls the container held.

After everything changed, Joya missed the querulous tones of her parents' arguments, Ma's voice rising above Baba's and vice versa, as each advocated what would be best for their daughter.

What neither would have predicted, she thought, was her daily walk to a garment factory near New Market, at a time her old classmates were cramming for examinations. The long walk left Joya tired. Even so, she would slide out of bed at night when the owls began hooting, and slip into the parlour, a bundle of loosely tacked rags in her hand.

Silence!

Choop-chaap!

Chaap-choop!

She marked the cloth with chalk, as she'd been taught in the factory, but the chalk wasn't for her eyes. Joya could feel the dusty dryness with the pads of her fingers. She allowed the powdery lines to guide her needle in the night gloom.

Her stitching had to be perfect. There could be no mistakes.

She was often tired the following day. After it became clear school was no longer an option, Joya forced herself to appear grateful when Shom Mamu, a distant relative, found work for her in his factory. But making clothes with speed and precision was challenging, especially if she'd had little sleep.

'Why your eyes are always red?' Lohith the manager demanded one day, hitting Joya's head, even though she hadn't yet made a mistake. 'You look like Kathakali dancer.'

Joya couldn't let anyone know about the suit she was making for her father. Especially her mother. Even though Joya had found a source for the material she used, and not a scrap of cloth had been stolen, perhaps she was stealing time from Shom Mamu by working her fingers raw at night.

And yet – how could something that felt so right be wrong?

Joya didn't answer the manager. He didn't want a reply.

Lohith walked away, pulling at the twisted cloth bunched between his legs, as if his dhuti pyjamas had a life of their own.

Joya tried to concentrate on the task in hand, but thoughts of the classroom floated into her consciousness when she saw the inch marks on the measuring scale. She remembered trigonometry, thought about the distance that had grown between Maia, Yusef and herself. What sort of triangle were the old friends forming now? She wondered how long the hypotenuse between the farthest points was. It was unlikely Yusef was still in the city. So many people had come and gone, some heading east, others west. Some stayed where they were, decaying by the side of the railroad. She wondered whether they could still form a triangle if one of them was already— But she pushed that thought aside and picked up more cloth.

She erased memories of school, blocked out thoughts about Maia, Yusef, trigonometry, fountain pens and calculus, and pushed yards of heavy twill through the machine to produce a perfect seam.

Five, four, three, two, one.

She counted down, as foot after foot of fabric went over the sewing machine's metal teeth. Sometimes the numbers danced in her head and bunched themselves into a different order. Joya had to ensure her mental acrobatics didn't lead to algebraic complications in the piece she was sewing. It was hard to remain focused on something so simple when her mind was used to walking the tightrope of the classroom.

Joya wondered whether she'd *ever* go back to school. How could she with Baba gone, when Ma needed every pice, anna and rupee to survive?

Lohith raised his stick.

'What this is?' He brought the lathi down onto the jagged line she'd made.

'A mistake, sir,' Joya replied with a trembling voice.

'Mistake is not permitted,' he said. The stick went up again and down onto Joya's fingers in a circular sweep.

Thwack.

Joya tried not to flinch.

'Undo,' the manager continued.

'I will.'

'It is wrong. Do you understand? Wrong is not permitted. Right?'

'Right,' Joya replied, swallowing her shame with the tears that had tracked to the back of her throat.

She undid the seam with an unpicking tool, and tried to calculate how many pices would be deducted from her wage.

One, two, three, four, five?

*

Since she'd started work, Joya had learned to perfect symmetrical shirt collars at a pace that didn't incur Lohith's wrath. The manager used a steel rule to correct tardy workers. He had a bamboo stick, his lathi, for those who weren't tidy. He wasn't too particular about matching the weapon to the misdemeanour, nor the severity of the punishment to the magnitude of the crime.

The factory's regime was very different from the orderly rules of the schoolroom. Universal truths didn't apply under Lohith's jurisdiction. Good behaviour had been rewarded at school, dereliction of duty punished. Right had been right and wrong was wrong. Plus was plus, minus was minus. No one, as far as she knew, greased anyone's palm to ease a journey.

Joya no longer looked at life through little-girl eyes. She tried not to think about schooldays, but when memories surfaced, they were bothersome yet irresistible, like scabs that must be picked.

The coefficients were changing: more irrational numbers and unexpected reciprocals. The direction her life was taking compared with the path she'd followed before resembled the asymptotes they'd studied in mathematics class.

In the factory, there was no consistency, no concept of fairness when it came to crime and punishment. And yet nothing was quite so unfair as her dismissal from school, punished for something she didn't do, couldn't have done, because she didn't know what the crime was.

These days, the rucksack came home at the end of the day containing the empty tiffin carrier and several scraps of fine material, almost too small to be of any use.

A Pen in Her Hand

Like the elves in the fairy tale, Joya did her best handiwork while others slept. Her fingers tugged on silky threads until they were taut. In the distance, midnight trains howled as they approached Howrah station. Nearer home, the *chirrup-chirrup-tip-tip-tip* of bats provided soft accompaniment to her thoughts as she worked.

How long. How long?

Will he ever return?

Quick! Quick!

The faster I finish his suit, the sooner I might see him.

But it must be tidy.

Must be the best.

In and out her needle moved, her stitches even, her finishing neat.

For months, Joya fell into a shallow slumber after supper. She'd wake to the sound of her mother shuffling into bed in the next room, and would creep into the parlour where Ma kept her scissors and threads, her iron and her pins. Ma took sewing in from friends and neighbours, and had taught Joya how to use the tools.

Like the fairy-tale characters, Joya's industry kept her awake, sometimes until dawn streaked the sky, only there was no shoemaker to appreciate her work.

Joya couldn't remember what the elves in the Brothers Grimm tale did during the day. Perhaps they slept. She, however, had a day of labour ahead.

With provincial elections looming, the factory workers had been discussing politics with raised voices and exclamations... *Chitter-chatter-shorbonaash!*

'What will become of Netaji's INA officers?' Pallav the machinist asked.

Whisper-shush-now-choop!

'Array baap-re!' Usman the sweeper said. 'But British are going soon, isn't it?'

Maybe-might-be-must-be!

'Officers are accused of treason,' Pallav continued.

Really? Hai-re-hai!

'My cousin-brother is in Indian National Army,' Bokul the cutter said, puffing with pride. 'He was fighting with wrong side before.'

Oh-oh-oh-oh!

Lohith tapped Bokul with his stick. 'Do we pay you for gossip?'

The chat continued regardless after the manager walked away, with talk of Congress and the Communist Party.

Political business.

Joya's belly contracted.

Had her parents been wrong to hide Baba's *political business* from her?

After everything changed, she wished she'd asked Baba about the *political business* when she could. Ma was a closed book on the subject.

Joya wished she were still at school. But that was impossible.

The factory's machines hummed and whizzed. Seeking something more probable, she wished she were home sewing with her own needle.

Joya cast her magic at night.

She didn't see with her eyes, but with her fingers: the occasional pinprick on skin, the needle feeding through gabardine and lining, the way the jacket took shape under her hands, how the lines were created that would eventually sit on her father's shoulders.

Uncle Shom's factory wasn't far from New Market, where high-class tailors cut cloth for the city's gentlemen. Joya had brokered deals with their managers. She collected tiny scraps, pieces too small even for their hands to fashion into useful garments. It made her smile to think Baba would wear the finest materials, that he would be dressed like a bhadralok, but in pieces.

As Joya stitched, she imagined how astonished Baba would be, if he ever came back, when she surprised him with her work. She had a good hand.

Master-Moshai had said her hand was like that of a noblewoman, that she could make uniform letters on her slate, the best in the class. The grey-haired headmaster had disagreed, saying Maia's handwriting was the most beautiful. Joya had been proud of her friend.

Working in near darkness, Joya took as much care turning her needle as she had with her pen. In and out, over and under, joining pieces together in the shape of a cuff or an epaulette. She hoped to see her father's freshly shaven face against the soft collar one day.

Joya didn't see Maia anymore. Her friend was lucky. She was still at school.

The new school building, Joya had heard, was equipped with a music room full of instruments: tabla drums, tambourines and a harmonium. There were lamps for murky winter days and electric fans for the fierce heat of summer.

Had things been different, she could have visited Maia.

But things were not different, and Joya knew better than to try.

Instead, she worked on her father's suit in the hope that when it was complete, things might change again, and she'd have a pen in her hand instead of a needle.

Hair Oil

Because the rains had washed roads away and drowned a little girl in the next street, Ma found Joya some money to catch the bus to work.

The pice coins burned in her hand. Money was tight.

Though she'd travelled by bus before, Joya had never done so alone. She didn't know what to ask for, or how she'd recognise her stop.

'Hurry!' the man behind her yelled. 'We don't have all day.' He shoved her. One of Joya's coins tinkled down the aisle. A lady wearing a green shalwar kameez caught the shrapnel with her chappal, bent over and grasped it with long fingernails. Joya held her breath, wondering whether the woman would keep her coin.

Everyone looked at her.

After much pushing and gesticulation, the money was handed directly to the driver, and a ticket was issued. There was nowhere to sit. Joya was manoeuvred between a tiny man with foul breath, and a woman with buck teeth.

When the bus careened around a corner, Joya grabbed the cord above her head to steady herself. She didn't connect her action with the urgent beeping that followed, and wondered why half the passengers were shouting or jeering. The bus screeched to a halt beside some derelict buildings. On the other side of the road were paddy fields and a lake.

'Array! Stop pulling the cord now,' the driver cried. 'I've stopped already. Who's coming off here?'

'Please sir, it's this girl,' a turbaned man said, pushing Joya through the crowds. On releasing the cord, the beeping ceased, and Joya realised her error.

'No, sir,' she said. 'I didn't know. The cord.'

She didn't know, several voices mocked.

'You are not alighting here, madam?'

'No, sir,' Joya shouted, so she could be heard over the din. 'I want New Market.'

An old lady dressed in a white sari squeezed against her companion, and pulled Joya onto the edge of their seat. 'Sit,' she said, 'and don't touch that thing again. I will say when we reach New Market.'

Joya balanced one egg of her bottom on the sliver of seat the woman offered. Someone stepped on her foot. She stifled a yell. The white-sari woman pulled her so close Joya could smell the oil in her hair.

Jabakusum.

Ma used to rub red hibiscus oil onto her head every morning. Recently, there were days she forgot.

Joya leaned in further and inhaled. She could almost taste the oil.

'Here it is,' the woman said. 'New Market.'

Joya was disappointed as she stepped onto the rain-soaked footpath. The white-sari woman waddled in the opposite direction.

Joya would have happily ridden the bus all day, inhaling the scent of her fellow passenger's hair oil, dreaming of her mother massaging her scalp with hibiscus.

Crying in the Night

There are times Joya hears her mother weeping at night. *Everyone should be asleep*, Joya thinks, *as indeed I should be*. She pushes a needle through cloth, imagines her father at the door, watching, approving.

She snips a thread, holds still, listening for the sound again, but it's gone.

Perhaps it's a wild animal.

Joya remembers a story her mother used to tell. It was one Joya's grandfather, Dadu, had told Ma and her sister Tiya Mashi when they were little. He'd told it to them when they were frightened by sounds after dark. Though Joya never questioned this when she was small, she wonders why parents would tell their children something so terrifying.

Long ago, Dadu used to say, when civets, mongooses and jackals roamed freely around the villages of the far, far south, night animals made friends with children who couldn't sleep. They'd wait until adults had closed their doors, thinking their sons and daughters were slumbering, and then they'd tap on the windows where the children waited.

'Chi-chi-chi-chi-chi. Chi-chi-chi-chi-cheeee,' the civets would chitter.

'Pupuchee, pupuchee. Pupucheeeee-chi-chi-chi,' the mongooses would chatter.

'Awoooooooo, awoooooeeeew, eeyoo-wooo!' the jackals would cry.

Ma and Joya would make the animal noises over and over. Then they'd lie back laughing, only continuing when Joya's mother had composed herself.

There was a boy called Biju, she'd say. His name meant *jewel*, and he was a precious child whom everyone loved. He had midnight-black hair and eyes that sparkled like stars. Biju was the youngest of seven brothers and sisters, and he was but seven years old when this tale took place. Biju was a well-mannered boy, who respected his elders and helped others whenever he could. He was closest to Anuradha, the youngest of his sisters.

His parents loved Biju for his good deeds and sweet nature, but there was one thing about him they would've changed if they could.

Biju *would not* sleep. After hours of lullabies, stories and gentle backstroking, he'd close his eyes and fake sleep, so his mother, father or Anuradha could creep away to their chores or their own bed.

The night animals came when the elders weren't listening.

Chi-chi-chi-chi-chi-chi-chi. Pupuchee, pupuchee. Awoooooooo.

When they tapped on his window, Biju would be ready, kurta over his head, chappals on his feet. He'd leap out to join his animal friends. They'd run to the jungle, jump into the river, swim its entire length and back, fly on the backs of night birds to the tops of mountains, and then return to the outskirts of the villages to climb the highest kadam trees and look down on a sleeping world.

Biju would feast with the night animals, his belly so full of fruit and seed he could eat nought but a tiny morsel on his return.

This continued until the child's eyelids grew thick for want of sleep. And still, the cry of the night creatures lured Biju from his bed.

Chi-chi-chi-chi-chi-chi-chi. Pupuchee, pupuchee. Awoooooooo.

The king of the jackals was known by the stout horn that sprouted from the middle of his forehead.

At this point, Joya would interrupt her mother.

'But Ma, jackals don't have horns!'

'Hush, child,' her mother would say. 'This one did.'

The king, Ma continued, had heard of this boy. It was said he believed the child must be gifted with special powers, since he existed in both the world of men and the realm of night animals. The animals whispered among themselves that the king sought Biju, as he wanted him to be his heir. The jackal king had no sons or daughters and it was said he would take an heir from a different world.

One night, a sharp tap came on Biju's window, followed by a cry that would have woken the dead, had they been listening.

Awoooooooooooooo, eeeeeeeew, eeeeeeeew, eeyoo-wooooooooooo!

Biju turned to look at Anuradha with a heavy heart. He knew who had come for him. And he knew he wanted to go. His eyelids were so heavy from lack of sleep he could barely make out the shapes of his siblings under their blankets in the faint moonlight. With one silent wave, he leaped out and joined the king.

The following day, Ma continued, the whole village gathered outside Biju's home, where the boy's family wept because their jewel-child was missing.

'How can we help?' the villagers asked. 'Shall we organise search parties to comb the jungle?'

They looked for seven days and nights, but not a trace of the boy was found.

At this point in the story, Ma would always pause. Joya would pout and say, 'It can't end like that!' She knew very well that it didn't finish that way, but she still said it every time, just as Ma and Tiya Mashi had to Dadu years earlier.

After what seemed like forever, Ma would continue.

Years later, when Anuradha was grown up with children of her own, she'd hear a tapping on the windows after her children had been put to bed. She'd rush outside to see who was there, but find no one. Sometimes she'd hear a faint *eeyoo-woooooooooooo* in the distance, and at other times, she'd hear nothing but taps.

One night, Anuradha lay waiting beside her youngest child, who was fast asleep. The night animals should leave sleeping children alone, she thought, and yet here was the tap-tap-tapping on the window. She crept out from under the mosquito net, tiptoed to the window.

Eeyoo-woooooooooooo! The call was faint at first.

Then again: *Eeyoo-woooooooooooo! Anu-Didi, is that you?*

In the moonlight, she saw a creature, half-man, half-jackal, with a horn in the centre of his head and eyes that shone like stars.

'Biju?' she cried out. But when she looked again, the hybrid man-animal had disappeared.

As a child, Joya had found the story intoxicating, because of its mystery. Now she cries in the night at the cruelty of it.

The Sash

Joya is clearing out her cupboards so dresses she has outgrown can be parcelled up for her younger cousins, when she finds a blue satin sash. Nothing else. No dress, just the sash alone. She remembers pujas from years ago.

Although it was her mother's job to prepare food, press the clothes, budget for gifts and arrange miniature shrines for every puja, Joya's father took great pride in dispensing colours for their Diwali rangoli.

'These patterns have been in our family for generations,' Baba said, reciting names of his ancestors, as if counting the beads on his mala for prayer. Since Joya had never known her paternal relatives, she was hungry for information about them, though Baba rarely revealed anything beyond the names of the string of Guho elders.

Joya loved watching her father work. First he made an outline in circular sweeps. Different coloured powders followed. Then he made simple floral shapes. Other motifs came next: peacocks, dancing women, or men banging drums. He'd drop powders onto the floor from his cupped hand and drag spoons or toothpicks through the mounds to create bicoloured petals or feathers.

A breeze from an open window, or a careless sweep from the hem of a sari could destroy the patterns, but somehow they stayed intact until puja was over. Ma didn't pour powders, but she'd add oil lamps to illuminate the designs.

The buttery smell of kaju barfi filled the house as Joya's mother prepared food for the forthcoming celebration.

'Is everything ready for the dance tomorrow?' Ma was careful not to disturb the patterns Baba was creating on the floor.

Preoccupied with rangoli patterns, Joya had forgotten she was supposed to make a sash for her dress. Ma had taught her to cut cloth and operate the sewing machine using the foot pedal. She'd be dancing with five other eleven-year-old girls. Her outfit was ready except for the sash.

She stayed up late that night, tacking, stitching, trimming, turning and pressing.

Joya takes the sash and folds it neatly. She wonders what happened to the dress. Perhaps it has gone, like so much else from her life.

Snakes and Other
Abominable Creatures

'Two women on your own,' Mary D'Costa says. 'And such troubled times.'

Joya peeps through a crack in the bathroom door at her mother's visitor. The woman is wearing a light raincoat. She hasn't removed it despite the damp patches on her shoulders. Joya herself has a towel wrapped around her hair, another around her body, and a neem kathi poking from her mouth. She chews the stick to splay its end, and works it across the surfaces of her molars.

Mary is the first visitor they've had for months. And such an early morning caller at that!

Very few people apart from the doodwallah come into the house anymore. He stays long enough to take the milk money, and then skitters away rattling his empty pans. Joya thinks she hears him breathe a sigh of relief as he leaves.

Since everything changed, it's as if Joya and her mother are lepers. The only difference is that they are allowed to go to their respective work places, but they must return to house arrest and isolation at the end of their shifts. Perhaps they are more like political prisoners.

Joya wonders why people are so hard on a widow and her unmarried daughter.

Mary accepts the tea Joya's mother offers, despite insisting on her arrival that she won't take anything. She doesn't wish to impose. She is so like Ma in this respect.

Never accept a gift without first refusing it.

Mary helps herself to a Thin Arrowroot biscuit from a plate. Ma hasn't purchased biscuits for months. Joya realises Mary must have brought them herself.

Joya towels her hair dry, applies the tiniest drop of Jabakusum oil. She doesn't wish to waste it, but if she is to appear before her mother's visitor, she wants something to counteract the taint of their exiled status.

Perhaps people don't believe Ma is really a widow, and who would blame them? The circumstances of Baba's disappearance are so mysterious Joya herself doesn't fully understand what happened.

The stigma of being an abandoned wife is something Mary is immune to, since she herself is divorced. Only Mary D'Costa is not an abandoned wife. It was *she* who abandoned Christopher D'Costa.

But Mary D'Costa is a woman of independent means. She can afford to make such decisions.

Joya dries the damp skin under her arms. The hair is growing thicker there.

Perhaps people don't stay away from them because Baba disappeared under mysterious circumstances, but instead because they fear Ma and Joya are infected by the same contagion. Maybe word has spread about the two-tailed snake, and though very few know who or what he is (Joya included), they know Officer Guho was involved in *something* that put his life at risk. They don't want to come too close, in case the snake comes back for more.

Joya can't help but remember Audrey Alvares when she sees Mary. Those two women, a little older than Ma, were her mother's friends in the days before everything changed. Both ladies were regular churchgoers. Both had extraordinarily long noses.

Joya remembers the gingerbread house Audrey Auntie made for her when she was little, and a rush of saliva embarrasses her. She closes the bathroom door a crack, as if Mary might detect the scent of her memories and feel pity. She spits out the medicinal-tasting neem kathi extract, and rinses her mouth to better savour her memory.

'And *they* wouldn't help you in any way?' Mary asks.

Joya wonders whom she is referring to. The police pensions department? Her father's absent family? One of the three hundred and thirty million deities that watch over the land? She pulls a crisply ironed shalwar kameez over her damp body and doesn't grasp what the two women say, until she hears her name spoken.

'Joya?' Her mother shouts. 'She is in the bathroom. She will come in just a minute. Let me call her again. Joya?'

Joya pretends she hasn't heard her mother. She's not ready to face the visitor yet. In twenty minutes or so, she must leave for the factory. If she loiters in the bathroom long enough, she can pare the encounter down to a few minutes. She sits on the bathroom floor, head on her knees.

Perhaps Joya's exile is partially self-imposed. She doesn't want to see Mary, even though she has known the woman for years. Mary is one of many people they used to see when visitors came and went at all hours, neighbourhood families and those from farther away, in the days when they had friends of every caste and creed. Joya straightens the cotton of her kameez, and notices a small hole over her midriff. She must mend that tonight before she works on the suit she is making for her father.

Ma and Mary are still discussing security. Ma mentions the door bolts and bars on the windows. They weren't cheap, but Joya feels very glad to have their protection when there are predators waiting to pounce on two isolated women.

Joya is annoyed with herself. She should face Mary. But isn't life hard enough without the need for insignificant talk? She has forgotten how. Entertaining guests seems so trivial, so irrelevant, when there are snakes and other abominable creatures marking the territory. These are troubled times.

Are venomous snakes worse than those that squeeze the life out of you? Perhaps the most dangerous ones are those with two legs and two arms that walk the earth as if they own it, squeezing blood from their victims, drip by drop by drip. Perhaps the worst of all is one with two tails, but Joya is still trying to deduce exactly what sort of creature that is. Warm- or cold-blooded? Or something else altogether?

She should greet Mary. The woman took such an interest in her schoolwork. She should offer a pronaam, and then leave.

The heat is stifling despite the rain. Joya doesn't feel well. If she could stay home she would. Except if she doesn't go to the factory, she may lose her job, and that would be a disaster, since she is no longer a schoolgirl, but a breadwinner.

She opens the door, forces a smile.

'How lovely to see you, Mary Auntie.' She bends to touch the lady's feet.

And it is. It really is lovely.

The Surprise

Joya and her mother swept the floors, wiped the walls, dusted fading lampshades, watered herbs and saag in the garden.

'I'm going to market now,' Ma said. 'Please bring me the shopping baskets from the almari.'

At fifteen, Joya could reach cupboards her mother was unable to. Already much taller than Ma, she wondered how much more she *could* grow. She'd inherited her mother's glassy eyes, but her height came from her father.

'Here you are.' She passed the wicker baskets to her mother.

'Why not come with me?' Ma cupped Joya's chin.

'Do you need help? Will there be much to carry?'

'No.' Her mother smiled. 'I want to buy you something special, shona-moni.'

Joya's face warmed at hearing the pet name. 'There's nothing I need.'

Lately, Joya's mother would write lists, calculate how much items cost, and then scratch some out with her pencil.

'It seems as if we have to pay for everything twice,' she'd complain. Joya's wage from the factory helped, but there was barely enough to survive on.

'Need and want are two different things.' Ma pinched Joya's cheek. 'You work hard. And in that factory of all places when I know you wanted to stay—'

'Why don't you buy something special for dinner?' Joya interrupted. She understood they were short of money. Leaving school had been a necessity. But she didn't want to discuss it. 'Bring something tasty we can enjoy together. I'll stay home. I'm tired.'

Joya had completed the waistband on her father's suit the night before. Working in the half-light, she'd traced the path her needle took with her fingers. One of the seams hadn't reached her exacting standards. She'd had to unpick it.

'What shall I fetch?' Ma asked.

'Ilish maach, if you can find it.' Joya's mouth watered. Hilsa fish was her favourite. The delicacy was deadly if a fine bone caught in your throat, but so succulent, it was an acceptable risk to take.

'Oh yes! Ilish!' Ma said. 'I've placed some yoghurt to set. Yoghurt goes very well with maach.'

*

Joya hadn't meant to fall asleep. The sky was darkening to the east when she woke. The baskets were bulging with onions, jhinga, dharosh and tomatoes the size of a fist. Such plenty reminded Joya of Maia's kitchen. She hadn't seen Maia or any of her school friends for a long time.

Why was there so much food? Were they having guests? Perhaps there was a puja she'd forgotten about. What had happened to Ma's frugality? The fish was marinating on the table, in a bowl with a glass lid. The pungent yet delicate spices made Joya want to tear into the raw flesh.

'Ma?' she called out.

She found her mother picking herbs outdoors.

'Ah! You're awake.' Ma rose, placing a hand on her daughter's shoulder.

'I should have cleaned the rice and cut potatoes.'

It was Joya's responsibility to remove husked grains and grit from the rice.

'No matter,' Ma said. 'You must rest when you are not on duty. Come inside. You'll be excited when you discover what I have for you.'

'But I already told you, Ma. I don't need anything!'

'Just wait!' Ma's wide smile showed her crooked teeth. 'Such a surprise!'

'Aw, Ma! Tell me what it is!' Joya liked being teased, though she pretended to be annoyed. 'Did you buy me a horse?'

'Better than a horse.'

'An elephant?'

'Even better.'

'I know. It's jhinga.'

Joya knew Ma had bought handfuls of the ridge gourds she loved so much. 'All for me,' she sang, pulling one from the basket. 'None for you, and none for...' She stopped short of mentioning her father.

'I *have* jhinga, but the surprise is even better!'

'What else can it be? I only see vegetables and fish. Unless you've hidden a large animal outdoors.'

'I have found a husband for you!'

Joya felt the blood drain from her face. She turned away from her mother. Of all the gifts Ma could give, this was one she least wanted. She went into the parlour, ignoring her mother's protestations.

And so it was that the following week, dressed in a splendid Banarasi sari, Joya boarded a rickshaw with her mother. They went to a leafy part of the city, not far from where Maia's uncle lived.

After hours of protest, Joya had been persuaded to attend on the understanding she could refuse the proposition should she find the potential groom unacceptable. They had devised a code. If she mentioned jhinga posto, her favourite ridge gourd and poppy seed dish, it would indicate she didn't like the man. Marriage was out of the question and her mother must withdraw as fast she could, without losing face.

The prospective husband was a policeman like Joya's father. He had bulging muscles that seemed to inflate his khaki uniform.

'Please be seated, Mrs Guho,' the potential groom's mother said.

Ma sank into an armchair. Joya sat on a sofa next to her, and felt as if she were falling into an abyss.

The Husband

Joya's mother had played the husband game since her daughter was a little child.

Ma would go to market. On her return, she'd pretend she'd found a suitable match. They'd discuss whether he was fair-skinned or dark, if he was tall or squat, clever with numbers or words. Baba would add that his future son-in-law would be hunchbacked, but that wouldn't matter, he'd say, because they could use the boy's spine as a coat stand.

Joya found it hard to imagine her father's coat on anyone else's back but Baba's own, whether they had a hump or not. She joined in their laughter regardless.

Sometimes Joya insisted they procure a *pair* of boys, perhaps twins, one for her, the other for Maia. Though as she grew older, she guessed Maia's family would require a better calibre of husband than anything Joya's family could procure.

Later the games had stopped being funny. Joya sensed more in their meaning.

Then the day came when the husband game was played not in jest, but in earnest, as if Ma were dealing a set of divination cards.

The potential groom's mother fussed around them.

'Some lemon water?' She looked over her shoulder, yelling, 'Ay, Nikhiler-Ma! Nimbu paani, quick smart for our guests. Rasgulla too. We can't have them starve.'

'Don't go to any trouble,' Ma said.

'No trouble. Are you cool enough? Move closer to the fan.'

This continued for some minutes, Ma refusing everything as decorum dictated, even the lemon water, though it was a hot day. Regardless, Nikhiler-Ma arrived with misted glasses and plates of sweets.

Eventually, the 'boy' spoke. He looked to be fifty-eight, rather than thirty-eight as the marriage broker had claimed.

'Does she cook?'

Joya had been instructed only to listen unless someone addressed her directly. Ma listed a menu of delights Joya could prepare. 'For fifteen years of age,' Ma continued, 'she has already mastered many dishes.'

Joya mulled over their potential age difference.

Thirty-eight minus fifteen. Twenty-three years. Joya didn't need calculus or any mathematical formula she'd learned at school to calculate the age gap. Her classes were becoming a distant memory, though she'd rarely missed a day before she was asked to leave school.

Fifty-eight minus fifteen. Forty-three.

What would they talk about? Would the policeman be strict with their children? Would Joya be left a young widow like the white-sari-clad ladies she saw at the mondir who looked as if they were wrapped in shrouds, ready to be consumed by flames of loneliness? She would be in her late twenties when he reached his seventies, if the sagginess of his jowls were an indicator of the man's true age.

The heat was oppressive. The heavy sari engulfed Joya like an eiderdown as she pondered her future, only partly aware of her mother's words.

'...she makes wonderful payesh with gur. Every day is a special occasion with her sweets. Joya's luchi are as round as a full moon, light and fluffy, and her rooti a perfect accompaniment for her begoon bhaja.'

Her mother may have been exaggerating, but the praise was uplifting.

'Very good, Mrs Guho,' the boy's father grunted. He hadn't said much until then, but his eyes had widened as if the possibility of acquiring an accomplished cook had piqued his interest. He popped a whole balushahi into his mouth, and appeared to swallow it intact. Joya wondered how he could be so enthusiastic about food, when he'd barely tasted the sweet, so rapid was its transit.

'And her jhinga posto comes from the gods...'

Jhinga posto? The code words they had pre-arranged! Only it was meant to be Joya who used them if she felt she couldn't marry the boy. Did Ma not approve of him? She seemed enthusiastic as she catalogued Joya's culinary repertoire. Had she forgotten the code?

'And she is an obedient girl?' The policeman twirled his moustache.

'Yes,' Ma cried, as if desperate to impress.

'And she knows how to behave? We don't like any clever-clever business,' Joya's prospective groom continued.

'Naturally,' Ma replied.

'Ma?' Joya interrupted.

'Choop!' Ma whispered, silencing her daughter with a sideways glance.

'Ma,' Joya continued clearly. 'Did you remember jhinga posto?'

'Yes, yes,' Ma countered. 'I've already told them it is divine.'

'But the *jhinga posto*,' Joya emphasised. She would have kicked Ma's ankle had they been sitting closer.

'...and aloor dom. Such potatoes. Your son will discover my daughter is very talented.' Ma turned her attention to the parents again.

As Joya had once said to Yusef before he disappeared, it wasn't as if she never wanted to marry. She'd said she didn't want to marry when she was too young. And if she *had* to marry, she didn't want someone like this character. She imagined a husband who would respect her, so love could grow. She remembered Maia's secret love, a poet with whom she'd exchanged letters for over a year before they met. Love needed a foundation.

The conversation turned to the boy's attributes. His promotions and awards, plentiful though they seemed, appeared to make the policeman himself uncomfortable.

'Splendid,' Ma said.

'And, of course, there is the matter of… Khokon.' The father spoke between mouthfuls of food.

'Oh yes?' Ma said. 'Who is Khokon?'

'No matter,' the mother replied. 'He will hardly be a problem for your daughter. Our grandson is a grown man himself.'

'Your son's nephew?' Ma asked. 'How good he is to take care of him.'

'Khokon is his son,' the father replied. 'From his first marriage.'

'I'm sorry,' Ma said, pulling her handbag towards her midriff. 'When did she die – your *other* daughter-in-law?'

'She is dead to us,' the boy's mother continued in a plaintive tone, 'but—'

Ma had heard enough.

Jhinga posto or no jhinga posto, no further excuses were needed beyond the fear of an approaching storm that took Joya and her mother away from that house in the leafy suburbs, never to return.

Joya didn't feel lonely that night when she rose to sew her father's suit. It seemed there were forces surrounding her, forces that would keep her safe.

The Market

The wicker shopping baskets waited on the table. These days, Joya's mother budgeted carefully, counting every rupee, anna and pice. She slipped the coins into her purse and washed her hands with soap. They were about to leave for the market when Ma became embroiled in an argument with the man who supplied milk.

For weeks, Ma had suspected the bluish white fluid in his pails was adulterated with water or something worse. Years earlier, their old neighbours had fallen ill after drinking bad milk from the market. Rukhsana had feared her husband and son would die after Faarooq and Yusef had vomited bile. Since then, Ma was extremely cautious about dairy products.

After much shouting and fist clenching, the man broke down. His best cow had died, he said. And she was so young, he wailed. There were children to feed, his wife was with child, water dripped into the house through a hole in the roof whenever it rained, they owed money to the moneylender, there was this to pay for, that needed replacing, and the other was about to break into pieces. The list continued like multiple verses of a song. Joya listened from the back room, door ajar. An unwritten rule stated she should not leave her mother alone when someone from outside spoke harsh words.

Ma brought the man indoors. She pulled a chair out, gestured for him to sit at the table. She pushed the shopping baskets aside, poured tea from the pot and put two shondesh on a plate. Joya slipped into the kitchen. The shondesh had been thin and watery, as had most of the milk-based foods they'd prepared recently. The milk hadn't formed proper curds. However, seeing the man eat something created from his produce offered reassurance. The milk, though diluted, was likely safe.

After the doodwallah left, Ma fretted because there wasn't enough time left for her to go to the market.

'I have to iron my work uniform,' she said. 'I cannot go on duty with a creased frock.'

The daughter of the sick lady Ma nursed insisted her staff dressed smartly. The *yes-madam-no-madam* and bottom-washing would once have shamed Joya's mother. Now it seemed her only concern was that her labours brought rice to the table, even if they left her with a dirty hand. Ma used to say, *Some filth sticks faster than others*. It had been one of her sayings, something she said when speaking about shame versus dignity. Ma didn't talk about those things anymore, just as she didn't discuss holidays and happiness. It was another thing that was different in the absence of Joya's father.

Joya herself wasn't working that day, a rarity of late. Shom Mamu's customers had been asking specifically for her handiwork. Men who preferred western designs admired her precise machine stitching. Though the fabrics weren't suited to the climate, many, her own father included, admired the cut, and chose the style for their winter garments. Longer hours at the factory meant Joya had less time to sew the suit she was making for Baba. She'd planned to work on it while her mother was on duty.

When Joya started making Baba's suit, she would work at night in the semi-dark. She'd enter the parlour after Ma went to bed. But with her mother's variable shifts, progress had slowed. The outfit would be completed soon, but one thing was certain: Joya's mother must not discover her daughter's work. That would challenge the carefully constructed lie Ma had told since Joya returned from Tiya Mashi's house.

If Ma saw the suit, she'd realise Joya didn't believe Baba was dead.

Although Joya wanted to challenge her mother, she couldn't risk upsetting her. There was a chance she was wrong, and all that was left of Baba was ash that had washed away in the holy river.

What about the shopping? Ma didn't need to ask. At fifteen, Joya knew how the household ran. She hooked the loop of Ma's purse around her wrist, and tucked it inside a fold of her kurta and then headed out.

Potatoes! Potatoes! Potatoes!

So many choices!

The temptation was to buy the cheapest, reserving funds for other items. But Joya knew the older, softer aloo would have had the eyes picked out. They'd likely turn to mush before the week ended. Joya turned the tubers in her hands, inspecting carefully before selecting. She headed to the older part of the market, not far from the stench of the slums, seeking dharosh and begoon. The weight of the potatoes cut into her arms. Joya should have bought okra and aubergine first, and purchased heavier items later. She was still learning.

After the vegetables were packed, Joya counted her coins and asked for the exact weight of rice the remaining amount would fetch. As she walked away, the shopping baskets felt as heavy as iron frying pans. She turned a corner, watched dust motes dance in a shaft of light. The weight of the goods slowed her pace.

She'd forgotten daal! Perhaps she could exchange some rice for lentils. Joya turned back, and that was when she saw him.

He froze on the spot, hesitated for a second, and then walked briskly in the other direction.

The man was dressed in greying rags. Not the crisply ironed cotton or gabardine he normally wore during the cooler seasons.

Joya wanted to shout *Baba!* But something stopped her. She didn't drop her baskets and run to him – the goods were too precious. Instead, she paced towards the gap between two buildings where the man had disappeared.

Gasping for breath, Joya arrived at the tight alleyway. But when she turned into it, the man had gone.

The wicker shopping baskets weighed heavily on her arms, but not as heavily as the weight of her sorrow.

Blood on Her Father's Shirt

Though the light was dim, Joya saw a dark stain blooming on the cloth and thought she'd pricked her finger with a needle. Yet she felt no pain.

She worked on her father's shirt in the murk of night, using all her senses to place the stitches where they belonged.

Her fingers to feel the warp and weft of the cloth she'd cut into shapes to cover Baba's shoulders, to follow the contours of his backbone and fit the nape of his neck.

Her nose to smell residual dye, to know the acid bite of colour and how different hues affected the depth of her stitches.

Her ears to know the squeak of each fibre as her needle parted it from the next.

She used the theatre screen of her eyelids to visualise the crook of her father's arms to create a perfect fit, remembering how wicker basket handles cut into his arms as they ran from the market after rushing to buy vegetables before a downpour, hoping to avoid the first rain of the season with its inherent dangers.

She used her tongue to sharpen the thread into a point.

She used her tongue to savour the memory of meals they had shared, words spoken freely before everything changed.

She used her tongue to taste changes in the atmosphere.

She used her tongue and
tasted blood.

Angry Words

A fierce wind battered the rosewood trees and woke her. Joya wanted to return to her dream: a beach at sunset, cockle shells and painted ladies, sharing jalebi, licking syrupy fingers. But as is often the case with dreams, the truth changes when retold.

Was the man handing her syrup-soaked sweets really Baba?

Or was it someone who only looked like her father?

Was it her nemesis the snake?

Joya needed to examine his face; her father or an impostor? But sleep eluded her. Why? She'd been awake until the owls themselves had stopped hooting. As if possessed, Joya had attached buttons to Baba's suit. A hand-stitched buttonhole for each – they must align correctly, or her efforts would be worthless.

The shutters rattled and shook.

The unease simmered and percolated into the muezzin's call. It invaded the radio broadcast that filtered through from a neighbour's house and wound its way around the syllables of Clement Attlee's name. It settled in the bosom of a beggarwoman feeding her naked child near the gutter, and the baby wailed and wailed.

Joya's annoyance followed her to the factory, and was reflected on the faces of workers standing near the entrance. Had they too been torn away from dreams by the wind?

It appeared people had greater concerns than broken sleep. They were knocking on the shuttered gates, some calling *Lohith! Lohith!* They stopped when the manager appeared and told them to go home.

'Why? Why we are to go home?' Bokul the cutter yelled.

'Choop!' Lohith screeched, raising his lathi above Bokul's head. 'For the sake of all gods, go!'

The crowd quietened, but wouldn't move.

'Go home.' The factory owner Shom joined his manager and entreated the workforce to leave.

'What about pay?' several voices asked.

'Go home,' Shom said. 'We'll see to pay later. I hear they may declare today a public holiday. Go now. Go.'

Joya was uncertain what to do. People spoke in hushed voices, but stayed where they were. Everyone was talking together. They pushed and pulled for answers, traded replies. Someone mentioned the new nation state. Another whispered about Nehru. A third asked about the Muslim League. A huddle of boys spoke of a hartal, a strike that could cripple production in the factory and elsewhere. An old woman worried about whether she'd have a job to return to afterwards. *After what?* Joya wondered. *When?* People whispered. Did someone mention a snake? Frightened voices warned others about danger. They cautioned and cajoled. *Go now! Be careful!* And then a scream cracked the air.

Before Baba's disappearance, Joya's parents rarely discussed politics with her. At dinner, they asked about school activities. Bombay films. Test cricket matches. Classmates. Had Joya imagined a lukewarm response when she mentioned her closest friend? Maia shared her secrets with Joya, secrets that threatened to burst out at times. Joya worried for her friend's safety, the wisdom of her choices. She'd come close to telling Ma and Baba about the poet Maia had fallen in love with, but had always stopped herself. And yet, it seemed they knew *something*.

Why had she worried about something so trivial, when disaster was brewing in the city?

She'd complained that the neighbours had left without a farewell.

'Yusef didn't even say goodbye,' she'd moaned, like a small child.

'Relocating is not easy,' Baba had replied.

'Rukhsana Khala was like your sister, Ma.'

Why hadn't she seen what was happening outside the tiny square of her life? Why had her parents protected her? She'd been almost fifteen, not a child.

Baba's work overlapped with *political business*, but Joya didn't know how. She'd sensed that the turbulence around them *might* boil into something urgent. Urgent, she'd thought, but not dangerous.

There had been clues:

How Baba kept two sets of newspapers, one by Hindu, the other by Muslim publishers. He read them both, but when Joya looked for them, there was no sign of either, except perhaps a sheet or two filled with advertisements found under the shoe-blacking brush.

How Baba didn't come home until late. His meetings became longer and longer.

How people appeared at the door, and were led to the back room by Ma, where there was barely a raised voice, but many an angry word spoken.

How those people, dressed in khadi, the homespun fabric that symbolised freedom, would appear for weeks then never return. Until Baba disappeared, Joya had thought *they* were safe.

The political situation was complex. Intangible.

But Joya understood danger in a very concrete way.

*

A soda bottle whizzed through the air and crashed on the footpath. The crowd moved, slowly at first, then running faster, faster, taking Joya with them. Then she was running alongside strangers. More screams. Was that a gunshot? Her legs weakened.

'Here! Quick!'

Bokul grabbed Joya's arm and pulled her into a building.

'We can't open again, bhai. More are coming?' An armed security guard pulled a bolt across the door.

'I don't know.' Bokul released Joya's arm. 'Go. Lie behind counter.' The blinds had been pulled closed.

Joya realised they were in the bank. She'd been in the building once with Baba when he'd deposited cash.

She stumbled, almost fell over the body, covering her mouth as disgust and fear rushed up with the vomit.

A boy.

He couldn't have been much older than her, the khadi torn from his body lying in tatters beside him.

It was hard to see in the gloom. More gunfire. Shouts.

There was a cut across the boy's face, ear to ear. It looked as if he were smiling.

A gigantic, grotesque smile.

Until that point, Joya thought her father's disappearance was the worst that could happen.

Now she realised there was worse.

Much worse.

A fierce wind blew outside.

Ratta-ratta-tatta-oooooooh.

Perhaps it wasn't the wind. Perhaps it was gunfire and incendiary devices.

It would be a long day. It would be a long night. Not a night for dreaming.

BEYOND THE WEEK
OF THE RIOTS

Award

At the front of the hall, blinking fast, Joya stems tears of happiness.

Maia is smiling, overflowing with pride. Joya steps onto the dais to accept the award from...

There's Master-Moshai, their old teacher, standing with open arms. He welcomes Joya to the head of the table.

'Show them some alphabets.'

Her chalk slides over the slate.

Orw-ahr-horshoi-diggoi.

'Well done, shona-moni,' her teacher says, but only Ma and Baba call her *shona-moni*, their gold, their pearl, their precious girl.

Master-Moshai wears a smile that resembles Joya's father's smile. He pins a rosette to her frock. The pin pierces so deep she might...

Joya is careful as she takes step after step to mount the stage at the front of the hall. Her chappals are loose. She fears she may slip. They are the wrong size because they are not her shoes. Aroti's feet grew too fast one summer, and she passed her sandals on to Joya.

But Aroti has a houseful of younger sisters – why did she give me her shoes?

And it is during this moment of lost concentration that Joya falls. The trapdoor opens as it must for the gallows to be effective, but instead of being hanged to death, Joya cartwheels into hell, where Lohith the manager from the factory, who has coins for eyes, beats her with a bamboo pole for not working fast enough, for she must finish her father's suit before, she must finish her father's suit before, must finish her father's suit before. Before what? And how did Lohith come to know she is making a suit for Baba? *Did the two-tailed snake tell him?*

Joya sews the suit at night from scraps she has stolen from Shom Mamu's shop, from beneath Lohith's unadulterated gaze.

No I never. No I never. No I never. I never stole anything.

The New Market tailors gave them to me.

Joya peels the caul from over her skull and walks out of...

Everyone is clapping. Applause for Joya, because she has won an award, the top award, the prize for integration and differentiation, though she once heard Baba say, *I find this whole caste business distasteful.*

Yes. So unnecessary, ogo, her mother had replied.

'Speech!'

'Speech!'

'Speech!'

They call for an acceptance speech.

'I...' she begins.

The judge lays her gavel on the bench and steps down.

'Why didn't you finish your father's suit?'

'I thought I was the one who asked the questions in this,' Joya replies.

'In what?'

'In *this*, whatever it is.'

'If you'd met your target, things might have been different,' the judge replies.

'I could finish it now,' Joya says, 'but the suit was supposed to be a secret. A surprise.'

'Very well,' the judge says. 'You have an extra day.'

'And a night?'

'One night?' The judge scratches her beard. 'I may not have the authority to grant a night.'

'I need the night.'

'Why haven't you finished it already?' the judge asks. 'You, who were so good at studying theorems of continuous change. Why?'

'I was angry.' Joya worries she might wake Ma, because the walls are thin.

'The walls in hell are thinner still,' the judge says.

'That's a lie,' Joya replies. She knows about hell's walls. She's so hot. Two familiar red-capped figures hover at the periphery of her vision. Her breathing comes faster, and Joya wonders if the elves that helped the shoemaker have descended into this tier of hell with her.

The judge's gavel pounds inside her ear.

It's so hot.

Didn't you know it was hot in hell?

The judge sneers as Joya screams. The judge has two tails.

*

'Shaat, shaat, shona-moni.' Ma wiped a moist gamcha across Joya's face.

'It's not true.' Joya tried to push her mother's hand away.

'What isn't true?' Ma asked, wiping the cloth over Joya's crisp-dry lips.

'I was in hell,' Joya said. 'I won an award. They sent me to hell.'

'Shhh, shaat.' Ma tried to shush her into silence. 'No one will send you anywhere.'

'Where did the judge go?' As the words slipped from Joya's lips, she realised there was no sense to them, and that whatever demon had brought this fever upon her would just as soon take away her powers of reasoning if she let it.

Shanti's Annaprashan

Three days had passed since the riots began. Joya's mother changed the dressing on her daughter's forehead and lay down on the bed beside her. It had been windy earlier in the day but the weather had settled. The air was warm, heavy with the promise of rain. Ma stroked Joya's head. The Mercurochrome stung. Joya wanted to wrap a length of Ma's hair around her finger, but resisted.

'I thought I'd lost you, shona-moni.' Ma used Joya's pet name, and quickly added, 'I couldn't bear to lose you both.' It sounded like an afterthought.

Joya wondered how long Ma would keep lying, why she spoke of *losing* Baba as if he was a misplaced toy. But was she suspecting Ma for no reason? After all, many spoke of departed loved ones that way, as if uttering the word *dead* would take their loved ones to a deeper level, further away from life. But Ma behaved like a widow in other ways. If Joya's father wasn't dead, why did her mother continue the charade of dressing in white? She wore the same sari when she wasn't in work uniform, washing yards of creamy cloth if rain wasn't a certainty, as it seemed to be that day.

If Ma was lying, where was Baba?

Joya was sure she had seen him in the old market. Or was she? What if the man only looked like her father? The low sun had been shining in her eyes. If it *had* been him, how could he be so cruel as to turn away from his only child? If it wasn't him, why had the man frozen to the spot and then scuttled away like a cockroach?

Perhaps it was time for Joya to voice her suspicions. She wasn't sure how to begin. 'Ma?'

'Yes?'

For a moment, Joya felt unable to continue. If Baba was really dead, it would be unbelievably cruel to ask whether he'd *truly* been reduced to ash on the banks of the Ganges. And yet... and yet, Joya hadn't *seen* his pyre. She'd been sent away to Tiya Mashi's house. But that hadn't happened immediately after Baba disappeared. Where had he been in the intervening days? Where was he when she'd been ousted from school, when Ma had only spoken in riddles?

'You know when Baba...' She hesitated.

'What, shona?'

'Nothing.' Joya couldn't say the words. 'It's nothing.' She couldn't do it.

Not yet.

'I know!' Ma exclaimed, as if she'd sensed her daughter venturing into dangerous territory. 'I'll make nimki!'

'There's no flour,' Joya interjected.

'I found some. I saved it in a tin and forgot.'

'But you can't heat oil in the dark. You'll burn yourself!'

'I'll light candles.'

Since Joya had returned from the riots they'd been living in semi-darkness, too scared to turn lights on when the power supply returned. Neither had ventured to work, each intimidated by shouting and the crash of breaking glass.

There were only a few scoops of rice left. Someone had stolen the saag and herbs from their garden. They shouldn't waste precious oil on a delicacy such as nimki, but the thought of the savoury treats made Joya's stomach dance. They'd eaten little but boiled rice with ghee for days.

'But first,' Ma said, 'let's listen to the news.' It was unusual for Ma to keep abreast of current affairs, let alone share them with her daughter. Joya suspected recent events had invaded their lives with such force they'd made her hungry for more information.

Ma turned the radiogram on at low volume. Sporadic episodes of violence were still erupting throughout the city. The Indian National Congress

Party, the announcer said, an organisation dominated by Hindus, was blaming the All-India Muslim League for inciting the riots. The Muslim League in turn felt those who supported Congress had been responsible for killing hundreds of followers of Islam.

'How can they be sure which is which when they are fighting?' Joya asked Ma when the broadcast ended. She'd heard stories about Hindu boys dressing as Muslims, speaking in exaggerated East Bengal accents in order to pass through areas dominated by non-Hindus. She guessed Muslim boys did the opposite.

'Oh, they know,' Ma replied, though she didn't elaborate on how.

When the first of the nimki came out of the pan, Joya put one into her mouth and spat it out immediately.

'Too hot!'

'Bōkā girl! Did you think they would be cold? Straight from the fire?'

Though Ma was scolding, Joya noticed her eager happiness. Her mother had been subdued since Joya had dropped through the door bleeding and bruised, tainted with the smell of death.

'I couldn't wait! I love nimki.'

'You always have.' Ma blew on a small triangle and popped it into her own mouth. 'Do you remember the first time you had it?'

'No. When?' Joya hoped Ma wasn't going to reminisce about a time they'd shared nimki with Baba. That would be too hard.

'Shanti's annaprashan.'

'How old was I?'

'Your cousin-sister was seven months. You would have been three years old.'

Joya remembered the trip to the west for her cousin's weaning ceremony – the first time rice would pass the baby's lips.

Stepping onto the train, Joya had nearly lost her father's hand. She'd feared she would slip through the gap between the carriage and platform.

When they arrived at Tiya Mashi's house, the cousins started running circles in the yard. Old Neha, who hadn't been so old then, had given them pans and wooden spoons to play with. Joya's spoon had snapped in two when she'd bashed it against an iron pot. She'd hidden the pieces.

The adults had been preoccupied because a bird had entered the roof space. They were trying to lure it out, tempting the creature with pieces of paratha. Baba poked the connecting skylight open with an umbrella and Mesho-Moshai threw his coat over the creature when it flew out, while Neha stifled her toothless giggles with a towel.

When the ceremony began, Joya had been permitted to offer the baby a spoonful of mashed rice sweetened with kheer, the milky smell so tempting she'd aimed the spoon at her own mouth instead.

'Na na na!' Ma had shouted, and directed her hand towards Shanti's parted lips.

Then Neha had fed Joya a nimki. It was delicious.

'When the doodwallah comes, may we make kheer?' Joya was craving the milk dessert since her urge for something savoury had been satisfied.

'I'll make anything you want when this madness is over,' Ma replied.

'When will it end?'

Joya hadn't expected a reply, so she broke the silence with another question.

'Tell me one of your earliest memories.'

'Let me think.' Ma sucked air through her crooked teeth. 'I remember screaming when a grasshopper settled on my frock.'

'How old were you.'

'Maybe two years.'

'I told Maia a story about a magic grasshopper once. I made it up.'

'Did she believe?'

'I don't think so. But I didn't believe hers.'

'What she did say?' Ma asked.

'Maia said she remembered being inside her mother's belly.'

'That girl speaks so much nonsense.'

Joya hadn't seen Maia since her father disappeared. Nonsense or not, she wondered if her friend was safe, and if they'd ever meet again.

They were living through difficult times. It was hard to know how things would end – or if the troubles would ever finish.

That was the way with uncertainty. It ate away at your core, Joya thought. She didn't know whether she'd see Maia or any of her old friends again. She didn't know whether they were dead or alive.

She wondered whether she'd live long enough to have children of her own and offer them their first mouthful of rice.

Her Father's Shirt and a Wet Newspaper

On her way back from the factory, Joya found a newspaper tucked behind a power transformer. Two days old, its edges were curling. Dodging a rickshaw that mounted the footpath, she took the paper home. Joya passed the rosewood trees, entered her house and double-bolted the door. She'd have to open the locks again before Ma returned after her late shift, but for the time being they would remain in place. She checked the barred windows for any sign of interference.

Joya and her mother had only dared venture back to work a few days earlier. The bloated bodies had not yet been cleared from the streets after the riots. They would have stayed home longer, but no work equalled no pay, and hungry bellies pushed people to do things they might otherwise not want to.

Ma's client, an old lady who lived with her son and haughty daughter-in-law, slept for most of the day, leaving those who nursed the woman after dark to do most of the cleaning, cajoling and comforting. Ma would be tired when she returned.

Joya's mother had left lentils and rice cooling in the larder. Joya added a scoop of rice to the pot of daal and ate from the pan without reheating her meal. Drips of yellow broth fell between her fingers. It was a steamy hot day, and she was hungry.

She washed the pans and set to work. Baba's shirt would need to be completed and hidden before Ma returned. There was only a double line of decorative stitching to do on either side of the centre, and the ensemble would be complete.

But first she wanted to read the newspaper.

The shirt could wait.

Joya wanted to know more about what had happened while they'd been hiding, details radio bulletins might have missed. The paper was water damaged, but the words still decipherable. She traced her finger over the rectilinear Roman script. The letters were very different from the curved Bengali calligraphy she knew so well.

Orw-ahr-horshoi-diggoi.

Although Joya had stood third in her English classes, it took multiple attempts to prise meaning from the longer sentences.

The headlines were not reassuring. Further rioting might ignite, extending the period of uncertainty beyond the week the papers first reported.

Various leaders had been interviewed.

Violence breeds violence

A city bent on destruction

International outrage

She turned the page to find more.

Human degradation

Uprooted and despoiled

Joya moved on to an article featuring an analysis of the recent violence and thuggery. What had initially been attributed to goondas and lunatics had in some cases been found to be orchestrated by middle-class politicians from the safety of their gated compounds. Political sloganeering pushed simple people to cut throats. Operators who never sullied their hands with blood were commandeering the gullible from behind closed doors.

There was so much more than she realised happening, not only in their city but in the whole country. For the first time, Joya grasped that her father may have been involved in something larger than she had realised. She recalled the partly heard conversations: public funding being redirected, washing dirty money clean, infiltrating the press, re-allocating contracts for government-funded projects to someone who was owed a favour, and the part politicians played in such things. Bodies in swamps, and the part politicians played in that as well. The people dressed in khadi who appeared at their home for weeks then never returned. The chaos and violence. The complex, intangible *political business* her father had been immersed in.

The article left Joya feeling uncomfortable.

She flicked through to the back to find an announcement for a dance programme. She suspected the troupe had already paid for publicity before the troubles escalated and weren't able to redact the advert in time. And yet, how wonderful it would be if they actually *were* performing. A ray of light in such troubled times. She'd heard in the recent war, there were parts of the world where entertainment continued even as bombs fell. People needed hope.

She needed hope.

Joya didn't know when or if her father would return. She missed him. But how wonderful it would be if she could cast those thoughts aside, even for a short time, if she could find something to make her smile. She missed Yusef's slow cackle, and Maia's high-pitched giggle. She wanted to laugh again.

Joya wanted to see Ma's crooked-toothed smile, her face devoid of worry. She threaded her needle and hoped such a day would come soon.

Urban Romance

'How were you and Baba introduced?'

Joya and her mother were peeling potatoes with thick knives, occasional skins falling to their feet.

'My Ma-Baba consulted a matchmaker. You know this story.'

Joya had no memory of either set of grandparents. She wasn't sure whether they'd died before she was born or if she'd been too young to remember them.

'How did they know my father would be right for *you*?'

Joya had been asking Ma about Baba in direct and indirect ways since the riots. She did so partly because her close brush with death heightened the need to honour his memory before that too might be lost. But it was also because she wanted to catch her mother out. Joya hoped Ma would let something slip, something that explained why, though they were always drastically short of money, they never ran out; something that explained why Ma always referred to Baba in oblique terms; something that made sense of the fact that she'd seen her father at the market.

'Your grandmother knew his people.' Ma launched into the story. It sounded familiar, like a poem Ma had learned by heart, and was required to recite to an audience. There were chaperoned visits to tourist attractions and central city eateries. Baba used to refer to this as their *urban romance*. He would smile when he said it, as if those words conveyed a secret joke only the two of them shared.

'When did you first love him?' Joya persisted.

'Why such funny questions?' Ma dropped a potato into the pan. 'When we've finished making aloor dom we'll take the bus to the mondir.'

Joya rarely used public transport. They usually walked to the temple, but the recent unease in the city meant even the overcrowded bus seemed less threatening than tackling the streets on foot. That was despite the paan-spitting men who swore and whistled at the ladies. Joya would wear her best clothes, and Ma her single white sari. They wouldn't want to spoil their kapoor by walking through muddy puddles.

'Yes,' Joya said. 'The bus is a good idea.'

She remembered a time she'd sat next to a woman on a bus who'd reminded her of Ma. It may have been the scent of the woman's hair oil. It may have been her kindness. She remembered how she had been comforted by the woman's proximity.

Safe. *Safer.*

That was the way she felt in her mother's presence.

Did Maia feel safe, wherever she was? Perhaps with her own mother and father. Maybe she was with her Boromama and Mamima. However, Joya couldn't imagine that man with his rotund belly and ineffectual eyeglasses being a comfort to anyone.

Was Yusef safe? Did Faarooq Uncle and Rukhsana Khala manage to keep him from harm? The thought almost made her choke with sadness.

Her mother did make her feel safer when she was there, even when she wasn't entirely truthful about Baba.

As they transferred cooked potatoes into the tiffin carrier, Joya wondered if she'd ever feel as safe as when she'd had both parents to protect her.

The Man at the Mondir

She saw him at the mondir as the pujari began to chant.

The words hypnotic and familiar:

OM NAMO BHAGAVATE VASUDEVAYA.

Closing her eyes and clasping her hands in prayer, Joya scolded herself. People didn't see the dead in the middle of the day – not within those holy walls, anyway.

The air was thick with incense.

As the words came again, Joya was lulled towards a sense of peace. She swore allegiance to higher powers, remembered the obligations she had to her mother and to all living beings.

On the third cycle of the mantra, she flicked her eyes open.

She saw him again at the edge of the congregation. He was looking at her, instead of directing his gaze towards the front as the others were. The air was smoke-filled, but she thought he could have been wearing the suit she'd made: a hundred shades of cloth carefully stitched together. Or it might have been a trick of the light.

Joya wanted to shout and swear like a street urchin at her mother for faking her father's death. She wanted to bunch up her sari and run after the man.

But when she looked away from her mother's eyes, pious and closed, the priest had started chanting OM NAMO for the fourth time, and Baba had gone, his back blending with all the others dressed in finery for the auspices of the occasion.

Transmigration

Joya was washing the rice. Her mother tossed poppy seeds into smoking oil. Their conversation continued above the crackles.

'I saw Baba.' Joya couldn't hold the thought in any longer.

'I see him too, shona-moni,' Ma replied dreamily. 'It is my fate.'

'No, Ma.' Joya slammed the pan down, spilled water onto the floor. 'I *saw* him. Flesh and blood.'

'You are imagining,' Ma said.

Joya wanted to stick thumbscrews on her mother's hands.

'I am not.' She spat the words out.

'You can't have seen him.' Ma spoke quietly.

'Why?'

The overcooked poppy seeds emitted acrid fumes. Ma threw slices of ridge gourd into the pan. Her crooked teeth made a caricature of her face.

'You have *not* seen him.'

'How do you know?' The steel in Joya's voice was sharp enough to cut flesh.

'You can't have,' Ma snapped, 'because Baba is not in this city.'

Joya grabbed her mother's arms, dug nails into flesh.

'Then where is he?' Her words came as a harsh whisper. 'What do you mean he's not in this city? Where did he go?'

'Baba has left his body.' Ma's voice was chant-like and hypnotic again, the anger evaporated. 'He is gone.'

The jhinga posto was burning.

Joya ran out of the room, slamming the door behind her.

Shraddha

She made shrines in unlikely places. Not having a son to perform the ceremonies, Joya's mother carried out the rites herself. Without them, Joya knew, a soul would not be admitted to their assembly of forefathers.

Some altars were hidden in cupboards or on tabletops in corners of this room or that. Others were in conspicuous places. Ma might light a dozen candles and dhoop kathi in the strip of land where they grew vegetables. After the rains washed everything clean, she might attach flowers to a street lamp on the footpath in front of their house, with a note containing a prayer or invocation.

Ma would kneel in front of her shrines and pray. Joya studied the curve of her skull, every bump and protrusion visible beneath Ma's freshly oiled hair.

Money had been in short supply, even with Joya and her mother both working, the pair of them squeezing in extra hours when they could. But women's work didn't attract as much pay as a man's. Joya had seen her mother count coins, place them in piles, this for coal, that for milk, this for rice, that for tax, nothing to spare.

Nothing for candles.

Nothing for incense.

Nothing for flowers.

Nothing for hibiscus hair oil.

Despite this, they always seemed to have enough of those things. Joya wondered how.

Not a word was spoken about the suit Joya had made for her father from thousands of fragments of cloth she'd secured from the New Market tailors.

Not a word was spoken about where Baba's soul was, and whether it would return to them. And if it did, Joya didn't know whether he'd come back as the father she'd known since childhood, or in the form of his next incarnation.

Someone Who
Looks Like Him

Yet again, she says she's seen her father.

Joya's mother doesn't believe her.

Once, she'd have been scared to tell her mother such things. Now, she wants to push Ma to the brink.

If she opens the wound wide enough, her mother will let something slip.

It's happened before.

'You can't have seen him,' Ma says.

'I did,' Joya counters.

'No. No, you did not.'

'But I did. I swear on my life, on your life, Ma.'

And so it carries on. For the most part, this is as far as it goes. Her mother complains of a headache and reaches into the wicker shopping basket for a piece of fruit. She pares the apple with a tiny knife, and Joya thinks of her cousin who lives far away, who likes apples so much she will consume two or three a day.

But she *saw* him. Or was it the light bending in unimaginable ways, fuelling her overactive imagination?

Joya's throat is thick with indignity as she swats flies away from the paratha cooling on the table. They have eaten two for lunch. Two remain for supper.

'You didn't see him,' Ma says.

'I did, I did.' Joya pushes.

Ma turns away, runs water into a basin. 'There is another who looks like him,' she whispers.

Ah! This is what Joya has been waiting for! She's pushed the stone away from the entrance, and now she can glimpse the cavern within.

'Who? Who, Ma?' She speaks softly, as if talking to a small child, coaxing them to admit a mistake they've made.

'No one,' her mother replies. But the djinn has escaped. Joya waits for the vapour of Ma's admission to diffuse through the small house.

'But you said…' Joya places the syllables carefully from tongue to tooth, to lip, to her mother's ears.

'I didn't say anything.'

Her mother bangs pots and pans. She peels a potato or two, back turned. Joya knows Ma is on the edge of tears. She is so close. All she has to do is listen, harvest the scraps and combine them with those she collected earlier. Piece everything together. She's good at doing that. This lie is too big to contain in this little house. The lie is larger than both of them.

'Only supposed to be for the shortest time,' Ma continues in a vicious whisper. 'Better she sees what everyone sees... Young tongues... Temporary arrangement. Huh!'

It is as if Ma has a fever. Troubled words spill like pus from a wound. Seeping. Weeping. Creeping through the air, as if they have a will of their own.

Joya remembers the time she had a fever, and how her mother wiped her face with a gamcha moistened with love. She loves her mother too, but this she must do. She rises from the table, places her hand on her mother's shoulder.

'What was temporary, Ma?'

'He looked just like one of them, they said, and so they sent him to do it.'

There are tears on Ma's cheeks. Joya soothes her mother with the softest of touches. For a moment, she is the parent, and Ma is the child.

'Who did he look like, Ma?'

'That girl speaks so much nonsense, and yet you go there to lick her bottom.' She sounds like a drunkard.

'What girl?'

'You didn't see anything.' And Ma is back again. Stone flags seal the chamber shut. She's gone. The mother-child has left the premises. In her place there is a strong woman, resolute, with a half-peeled potato in her hand.

Joya dashes a plate of vegetables onto the stone of the kitchen floor.

For days afterwards, she picks splinters from her feet.

The smoke settles. She rekindles the debate.

'I saw Baba again.'

'Did you *really* see him? How could you have done?' Ma says. Her mouth is a straight line of anger.

'I did see him.'

'People can look like the shadows of others.'

'What do you mean, Ma?'

Joya's mother's voice collapses into a whisper. 'Ogo? Why did you do it?'

'Do what?'

'He was supposed to confiscate the criminal proceeds.'

'What did he do instead?'

'Then he gets involved with this and that.'

'With what, Ma?'

'He was supposed to be investigating how they made dirty money clean. A good desk job. Huh! Look what happens when you dig too far.'

'And then what, Ma?'

'Nothing.'

Joya's mother snaps her mouth closed like a purse. But she has already said too much.

Little Hanuman

Though Joya's life had changed since she'd last visited, she knew the house well. The stone serpents that graced the archway once scared Yusef, but had seemed whimsical to her. Now their ruby-eyed stare made her uneasy.

Joya explained her business to the turbaned guard, who allowed her to slip the factory bicycle into the compound. The packages in the bike's panniers were heavy, and she worried the contents would spill onto the mud and be ruined. Lugging bundles of freshly tailored shirts up the marble steps, she wondered if she'd see the people of the house. Someone vaguely familiar was sweeping the gully at the side.

Joya had never delivered clothes before. Usually those who cut cloth in the factory only cut cloth. Those who sewed pieces did only that. Those who swept lint from the floor and oiled machines only swept lint and oiled machines. Suresh and Nitesh only delivered orders.

That morning, Lohith had asked if anyone could ride a bicycle.

Proud that her cousins had taught her when she was younger, Joya stood up without considering why the manager wanted to know such a thing.

'Me, sir. I can ride a bicycle.'

'You?'

'Yes,' Joya said. Looking around, she discovered no one else had volunteered, even though one of the cutters cycled to and from the factory every day.

'Come with me.' Lohith directed Joya from her sewing station to the tiny booth he referred to as his *offish*.

'Suresh and Nitesh are ill,' he grumbled. 'Today they celebrate a festival in their gram. Coincidental, I am sure.' His tone suggested he thought their absence coming at the same time as a celebration in their village was anything but a coincidence.

Joya said nothing.

'I need someone to take these to a customer.' He pointed to two bundles and showed her an address. 'Not far from here. Near Vikat's Emporium of Sweets. You know where is this?'

'Yes, I know it well, sir.'

'We can't ask these haramjada rickshaw-wallahs. What they don't steal, they'll cover with oil and shit.'

'Oil and... everything,' Joya repeated solemnly.

'Go now.'

And that was how Joya came to be at Maia's uncle's house.

Though it had been over a year, stepping into the entrance hall with its twin marble staircases felt like returning home. Joya struggled to recognise the servants who dashed back and forth.

'Wait here,' a skinny maid said. 'I'll fetch someone to check the delivery.'

A pillowy cat rubbed against her leg. Joya wanted to rub its chin as Maia had shown her.

They don't bite, silly.

But she couldn't put the packages down. She wondered how long she'd have to wait. Lohith had been clear. She was to return before tiffin time. The muffled clang of puja bells and the waft of incense suggested someone was performing a ritual nearby.

A wiry woman arrived, took the packages and dismissed Joya, who remained rooted to the spot.

'Go now, girl. Why you are waiting? A tip?' To her astonishment, the woman shifted both packs to one arm and produced two coins, which she pressed into Joya's palm. Feeling shy, Joya wanted to look away, but forced herself to respond by folding her hands in a gesture of thanks. Would she be scolded for taking a tip? Was the money hers to keep? Would anyone else know?

Before she'd had time to secrete the coins, a familiar form approached from the left hand staircase. Once again, Joya felt unable to move. Maia's Boromama appeared larger than she remembered. He supported his weight on an ornate walking cane. There was no greeting smile, no adjusting the distance of his spectacles from his face to gain a better view. There was little indication her friend's uncle recognised her at all, even when he was so close she could smell the tang of his cologne.

Joya wondered whether the old man would cup her chin as he used to when he realised who she was. But he never did. Instead, Boromama walked towards the exit, and Joya followed him out, not knowing whether she was disappointed or relieved that he hadn't acknowledged her.

Joya wheeled the delivery bicycle out of the gates to the side of the house. The adjacent swamp had been drained. Remembering how she'd played kabaddi with Maia and her cousins made her think she should have asked after her friend.

What was Maia doing?

Was she married? What had become of her poet-lover?

Would she go to college?

Did she have new friends?

But perhaps it was best she'd not asked after her. The world had changed since she and Maia had been friends, and so had Joya herself.

She pushed the bike onto the road and the jangling bells grew louder.

A child sat with its mother in front of a white building, begging bowl in hand. The mother was dressed in a threadbare sari.

'Give pices. Ensure good fortune,' the woman said, pushing the child forward. The baby was dressed in red pantaloons and a golden headdress. He wore gilt bangles and a necklace, and had a large mouth painted over his own with red sindoor.

'Array! You want to see miracle or not?'

'Yes,' Joya said, realising she'd been staring too long. She needed to pay.

'An incarnation of Hanuman himself,' the woman added.

Joya leaned the bicycle against a wall and parted with a coin she could ill afford to lose. But here was the monkey god, right in front of her.

The mother stood the child up and pressed her palms together in acknowledgement. She turned the boy around, pulled at his clothing.

He had a tail.

Joya gasped! She extended her hand to touch the fleshy appendage, but the woman pulled the child away.

'Touching costs more. But for more, I will also tell fortune.'

Joya worried Lohith would scold her for being late, but she couldn't leave. She passed the second coin over.

The tail was smooth. It yielded under her fingers and the child whimpered. Joya had expected it to be sinewy, perhaps covered in hairs, like a cat's nose.

'You will see him again,' the mother said.

'It's not possible,' Joya replied. 'I have very little money.'

'No. You will see *him* again,' the woman said. The child slid a thumb into his mouth. 'One who is dressed in a thousand pieces.'

'Who? Baba?' Joya hadn't seen her father for a year, a year in which her mother had behaved as if he were dead.

'That is all.'

'More! Tell me more,' Joya begged, but Little Hanuman began to cry, and the woman offered him her sindoor-smeared breast, dismissing her customer.

Joya pedalled to the factory, tears blurring her vision.

It wouldn't matter if Lohith scolded her for tardiness.

Joya had witnessed a miracle.

Ananta

Ananta, a coiled serpent, possesses a beginning but is without end.

The most powerful gods lie over Ananta's body. They become one.

When Ananta is worshipped on the night of Nag Panchami along with his sub-pantheon of snake siblings, he bestows good fortune on his devotees.

Ananta the all-seeing gazes into the future with one eye, reviews the past with the other.

Here is a witness who has learned to hold his face still: a visage unbent by lies. He has the skill of a Kathakali dancer. He can smile with one side of his face while the other cries.

Some say Ananta has ten heads, others a million. Some call him Ananta-Shesha. Some see a thousand heads. The snake-god swims through the milk ocean, supporting the weight of the world.

Ananta circles the earth, which has a beginning but is without end.

Here is a girl sewing minute stitches in the dark. Fatherless. Ananta watches.

Ananta has the eyes of a god, sees the unseen, smells the unscented and hears those who have lost the power of speech. For Ananta knows powerful speech creates tidal movements in one direction or another.

Here is a candidate for the legislative council who pays cash for votes, a few pice here, and some anna there. Ananta sees it all. The money comes from one hand before being placed into another, and is later transferred indirectly to one with both tails clenched over an overflowing mountain of gold. Ananta writes it in a ledger.

A higher-denomination note is removed from circulation in the hope of stemming black money. But Ananta sees the future, too, knows one day such blunt instruments will be put to different use.

Ananta sees the knot of bureaucracy tighten, a stranglehold that immobilises and stifles.

A headmaster wrings his hands at the thought of splendour. Ananta circles the man, who is surrounded by musical instruments: tabla drums, tambourines and a harmonium. He keeps lamps and electric fans meant for his charges. The man measures how fast his belly grows, pregnant with money syphoned from welfare schemes and donations.

This grey-haired headmaster once disagreed with another teacher about which student's handwriting was the most elegant. Some believe gods never notice little things, but Ananta sees, unable to change the wing beat of every moth, every feather, every scale, but seeing it all.

Here is Kāliya, a five-headed snake, inert in a river home. Kāliya is a demon who terrifies younger, benign deities. It takes a powerful god to subdue such a nāga, a snake-god bent on evil. Ananta waits as black water flows through the River Yamunā, washing Kāliya's five heads, sinking into the underground economy.

Here is a head constable of a police outpost who turns a blind eye to the slithering serpents in his district and orders officers to approach dangers he will not face himself.

He nominates an officer who looks like a felon they've watched for months, tells him to infiltrate, but warns he *mustn't get too close*. Ananta hears those fateful words, but can no more change the future than the past.

Here are three cats, faces like squashed balushahi, like bread-flour sweets deep-fried in ghee. Ananta has no disagreement with these purebred animals, but sees the owner's rival capture each one and take them into the murk of the night where they are drowned separately, each furred body thrown in a swamp.

Ananta knows those who are wronged strike at inert victims, because hitting the heart of the reptile carries the risk of venom or suffocation, a bullet or a disappearance, or worse, the disappearance of a loved one.

Ananta overhears someone ordered to replace the sweet darlings. The man looks like the father of a girl with beautiful handwriting, though he is thinner. He is sent to purchase other balushahi cats, matching them to photographs of the originals, to create an illusion they have been brought back to life. He almost succeeds, but cannot find three that are fat enough. Ananta sees the substitutes fed chicken fat before they are allowed to roam freely.

Here is a girl, crying for her father, her fingers thickened by pinpricks and industry.

The disappearance of a loved one is more painful than any blow or deprivation; worse than venom, suffocation or a bullet.

Ananta sees the great and the small. Ananta sees it all. Gods may have the power to do more than mortals believe. Or they may have less.

But Ananta knows what is coming. Mankind doesn't yet know how arbitrary lines drawn by a Viscount Radcliffe will cause the nation to crack.

Ananta circles the world, smiling and weeping simultaneously.

Headlines

OM NAMO BHAGAVATE VASUDEVAYA.

They left for the temple to give thanks after a khadi-wearing man brought the news. They walked against a tide of people moving this way and that. The chanting grew as they drew closer. Incense washed the air. Its essence settled in Joya's hair and percolated through her bones.

She held her mother's hand. They crouched to remove their chappals. Her mother had tears in her eyes. A train whistled in the distance. Another train would blow into their lives later that day to change everything. Again.

For the first time in over a year, Joya cried from happiness, the salt from these tears sweeter than those she had shed for so long. They washed the stains left from crying over her needlework, tears that fell as she made a suit from a thousand pieces for her father, refusing to believe what everyone said.

She would give special thanks to Hanuman.

Did she imagine the words she overheard? Was everyone was talking about what had happened?

Did you hear, Dada? They have captured the leader – the jemadar.

Did you hear, Bhai? They have arrested the whole gang, to the lowest goonda.

Did you hear, Boudi? You will no longer find those goods on the black market.

Did you hear, Didi? One school headmaster took bribes.

Did you hear, Choto Mama? The leader lived in a mansion guarded by two stone serpents, woven together as if they were one creature.

Did you hear, Dadu? Undercover officers in hiding can return. Some who were captured have been released.

Did you hear, Mashi? Today is a day to rejoice!

The news would make the headlines that day, and soon afterwards, most people would forget. Perhaps the black market would recover. It always had before.

But for this day, even if it were one day alone, Joya's hope was kindled.

Snakes III

So you thought he might get away with it?

To be brutally honest, so did I.

After all, that snake's spheres of influence had music of their own, though only those who knew could hear it.

And such a song it was:

An isosceles of hierarchies,
A theorem of prayer,
Proportionality that required no proof.

Poetic! Like something his niece's lover might write, though everyone thinks no one knows about Michael Smith, when we all do.

The snake had so many followers. It helped that one was a schoolteacher, of course. But what has become of him now?

Ah-ha-ha-ha-array! Do not pity him. Perhaps he will rise again. He always has before. After all, doesn't that particular snake only dwell in the Martya-loka, the plane of mortals, on a part-time basis? Otherwise, he is up there with Ananta and the good guys, pretending to be one.

Can prison bars hold one such as he?

Will he not slither through the bars and disappear? Perhaps. I hope so.

And what do I care whether the two-tailed snake is a free man or locked away until his bones rot?

I care very much. You see, I am not as indifferent as I've made out. I may have lied a little. My tails twitch with shame.

They truly do.

Though I might be lying again.

I have a sweet tooth.

I enjoy the balushahis you can buy at Vikat's Emporium of Sweets.

Are such things not indigestible to snakes, I hear you ask? Why, yes. But consider this: what might be poison for one snake may be manna from the heavens for another. I enjoy simple disaccharide pleasures, and take comfort in my pet animals, though none are dispensable, just like my goondas, some of whom made it to freedom. Others are locked here with me.

Hai Bhagavan!

I should say *him*, not *me*!

Homecoming

Joya's mother lays balushahi and jalebi on the table. She cups her daughter's face in her hands.

'I've made celebratory sweets,' Ma says. 'We've waited so long.'

They've seen many changes. Greater change lies ahead.

They've seen gods and miracles. Some events cannot be explained. Others are impossible. Sometimes the impossible becomes possible.

Ma asks Joya to peel potatoes she's harvested. So long underground, so long in the making. Joya finally understands why Ma hid the truth so long. She buried it like those dormant vegetables. Joya should be angry. But it's a day of celebration. How can she bear any animosity towards her mother when her father is returning?

Ma and Baba will share rice with their child.

Joya prepares the meal, fragrant spices in oil, and thinks Bhagavan dwells in strange places. The gods lie in spaces between things, in the expected and the unexpected, in the past, in the present and in the future, if her family is blessed.

There were times Joya believed she'd never see her father again. The best she'd hoped for was that he might be returned in an urn. There were times she thought he'd never wear the suit she'd made from a thousand pieces.

But here he is, a marigold in his outstretched palm.

Joya touches his feet, offers blessings in the form of a pronaam. When they embrace, she smells hibiscus oil.

Coals burn in the brazier.

The potatoes cook to a crisp.

Joya has blackened ghee on the back of a spoon. She anoints her father's eyes with the kajol she has made, adds clarity rather than darkening the space between them. She hands him a parcel.

The paper is filigree-soft, crumbling, incomplete in places. Baba unwraps the suit, its lines and folds as familiar to Joya as her own hands.

He emerges later dressed in it. Joya's measurements based on clothes in Baba's wardrobe and intuition have resulted in a perfect fit. The quality of the cut and beauty of the cloth astonish Ma.

'You never stopped believing,' she says.

Every fragment brings memories of late nights, tired fingers, the cries of owls and other night creatures.

They weep and they talk.

Baba tells her why he went into hiding. He says he wishes things could have been different.

He tells her she will leave the factory – go back to school.

She asks where. Asks if she'll attend the new school with its tambourines and drums, the school her friends went to. She is desperate to see her old friends.

'Yes,' he says. 'I will organise it in the morning.'

He tells her about the underground organisation he has been investigating.

Joya listens in silence as he names the ringleader.

He tells her great changes lie ahead.

She asks if they will be safe.

He tells her the two-tailed snake has gone.

Can corruption be eradicated?

No one knows.

But at that moment, it doesn't matter.

Baba is finally home.

Acknowledgements

Eileen Merriman, a guiding light who illuminates the path to better writing.

Nancy Stohlman, who hosts the annual 'Flash Nano' event, where writers of very short stories congregate online and produce a story a day to a given prompt. This book was written during the November 2021 event. Thanks, too, to the members of the Flash Nano community for encouragement, support and guest prompts. Some prompts took Joya and her friends in unexpected directions, for which I am grateful, though I was perplexed at the time.

My family on the Ghosh and Basu sides, who lived through times depicted in this story and shared their experiences with me.

Sarah Shaw and Laura Shanahan at Fairlight Books, for taking the bones of this work and making it into something better.

Bookclub and writers' circle notes for the
Fairlight Moderns can be found at
www.fairlightmoderns.com

Share your thoughts about the book
with #TheTwoTailedSnake

Also in the Fairlight Moderns series